WHITE

DENI ELLIS BÉCHARD

with an afterword by

Simisola Batta

MILKWEED EDITIONS

Published 2018 by Milkweed Editions
Printed in Canada
Cover design by Mary Austin Speaker
18 19 20 21 22 5 4 3 2 1
First Edition

Milkweed Editions, an independent nonprofit publisher, gratefully acknowledges sustaining support from the Jerome Foundation; the Lindquist & Vennum Foundation; the McKnight Foundation; the National Endowment for the Arts; the Target Foundation; and other generous contributions from foundations, corporations, and individuals. Also, this activity is made possible by the voters of Minnesota through a Minnesota State Arts Board Operating Support grant, thanks to a legislative appropriation from the arts and cultural heritage fund, and a grant from Wells Fargo. For a full listing of Milkweed Editions supporters, please visit milkweed.org.

Names: Béchard, Deni Ellis, 1974- author.
Title: White : a novel / Deni Ellis Béchard.
Description: First edition. | Minneapolis, Minnesota : Milkweed Editions, [2018]
Identifiers: LCCN 2017051227 (print) | LCCN 2017054897 (ebook) | ISBN 9781571319470 (ebook) | ISBN 9781571311252 (paper : alk. paper)
Classification: LCC PR9199.4.B443 (ebook) | LCC PR9199.4.B443 W48 2018 (print) | DDC 813/.6--dc23
LC record available at https://lccn.loc.gov/2017051227

Milkweed Editions is committed to ecological stewardship. We strive to align our book production practices with this principle, and to reduce the impact of our operations in the environment. We are a member of the Green Press Initiative, a nonprofit coalition of publishers, manufacturers, and authors working to protect the world's endangered forests and conserve natural resources. *White* was printed on acid-free 100% postconsumer-waste paper by Friesens Corporation.

The world had prepared no place for you, and if the world had its way, no place would ever exist. Now, this is true for everyone, but, in the case of a Negro, this truth is absolutely naked: if he deludes himself about it, he will die. This is not the way this truth presents itself to white men, who believe the world is theirs and who, albeit unconsciously, expect the world to help them in the achievement of their identity. But the world does not do this—for anyone; the world is not interested in anyone's identity. And, therefore, the anguish which can overtake a white man comes in the middle of his life, when he must make the almost inconceivable effort to divest himself of everything he has ever expected or believed, when he must take himself apart and put himself together again, walking out of the world, into limbo, or into what certainly looks like limbo.

—JAMES BALDWIN,
NOBODY KNOWS MY NAME

I was cut to the quick at the idea of having lost the inestimable privilege of listening to the gifted Kurtz. Of course I was wrong. The privilege was waiting for me. Oh yes, I heard more than enough. And I was right, too. A voice. He was very little more than a voice. And I heard—him—it—this voice—other voices—all of them were so little more than voices—and the memory of that time itself lingers around me, impalpable, like a dying vibration of one immense jabber, silly, atrocious, sordid, savage, or simply mean, without any kind of sense.

—JOSEPH CONRAD,
HEART OF DARKNESS

WHITE

I

SOLA

I *crossed the ocean on the blade of a knife.*

I read this line on the phone she held between us as she spoke it, slowly, and then said, "It sounds contrived to me, not at all the words of a child . . ."

This is how I met Sola, high above the Atlantic. When I'd boarded, she'd had an eye mask on, its elastic holding her dark, loosely curled hair in place, and during the flight's first hours, she'd slept by the window, an empty seat between us. Her mouth and the tip of her nose were visible, her lips slightly full and her skin a shade lighter than gold, almost flaxen.

As passengers lapsed into sleep, I remained restless. A hostess passed through the unlit cabin, balancing a tray of plastic cups, and I took one to wash down my malaria pill, and then I read. Sometime after midnight, I unbuckled myself and made my way back through the half-reclined bodies whose postures of disturbed repose gave me the impression that I was in the sickbay of a ship.

On my return, I paused to take stock of who was there.

The sleepers' jaws conveyed unease—heaviness, futility, even sadness—or were disconnected, dropped like a burden. I felt grateful to return to hers, her mouth that, resting, retained its dignity, if somewhat severe. And yet this impulse gave me pause: how even on the half-covered face of a stranger, the mind begins to compose.

I was considering a nap when she reached up to her mask and looked at me from beyond the domain of my reading light, her eyes too reflective to disclose the nuance of their color.

"You don't sleep well on planes?" she asked, and I wondered if her question was a way of telling me that I had awakened her.

"I can't blame air transportation for my sleep problems," I said.

"Is Belgium your final destination?"

"No. The Congo."

"Congo–Kinshasa?" Her voice was pleasingly neutral, its accent American but faintly bookish—more considered than automatic, so possibly an acquisition and not a birthright.

"Yes."

"Me too."

"Oh, what for?" I asked, resisting the temptation to articulate a synchronicity. We were flying from DC to Brussels, the Congo's old colonial warden, so obviously many of the passengers shared our route.

"It's a strange story," she said. "I don't want to interrupt your reading."

"My reading can wait. I'm all ears," I told her, though I normally shunned conversation in flight, for fear of losing anonymity, of having to be attentive to a stranger.

"Well," she said and appeared to gather her thoughts. "Someone I know—an anthropologist—he works with street children in Kinshasa and has found a white child, not an albino, but a blond, blue-eyed girl who speaks Lingala and the usual bits of street French."

"How old is she?" I asked.

"Maybe twelve, possibly thirteen."

"So you're going to help repatriate her to wherever she's from?"

"There's more to it. The girl believes she's black—that she's Congolese by birth—but that a demon—a white demon, according to her—has possessed her and turned her white."

That was when Sola reached up, adjusted her reading lamp in its orbit, and turned it on. She opened her bag and took out her phone. Then she lifted her armrest, shifted partially into the empty seat, and positioned the screen so that we could both read.

I crossed the ocean on the blade of a knife, the e-mail began without salutation, clearly one of many messages in a thread. *Each time we take a break from talking and start again, the girl repeats this line. I ask why, whether she believes she came to Kinshasa on a knife, and she says no, that she was born here, that her family are Congolese. The line, she says, is the demon's memory. The white demon rode on a knife to Kin and used it to cut open her heart so that he could live inside her.*

I paused from reading to meet her gaze—her irises were nearly sepia, with a thin bright rim of black—to confirm it was okay that I continue, and she nodded.

The girl's way of speaking is nonlinear and dualistic. The demon inhabits her and she embodies its power, and yet she is also its victim, fleeing it as she tries to find ways to kill it and win her freedom. She claims that she has no parents and yet that she was born in Congo. She doesn't verbally respond to English, but when I tell her in English that I have hidden a treat for her in the room, she gets it as soon as I leave. This doesn't work with other languages, except French, but her French bears no European inflections. It was clearly learned in the streets of Kin. Since her arrival in my care, I have dropped my other projects. I must confess that I have developed a possibly unhealthy fascination with her story.

"He's somewhat dramatic," I said before I could catch myself.

"Yes, he is. It's why this appeals to him. It's also why I'm going to help out."

I read the final paragraphs—a maudlin edge in his words about how long he'd searched and how much he deserved this breakthrough.

"And situations like these," I asked, "they're related to your work?"

"I've done time in many fields, but I sell myself as a cross-cultural consultant."

"That's why he contacted you?"

"No. He's a personal connection—one that," she took a moment to renew the air in her lungs, "I have been doing my best to manage from a distance. But a friend is a friend. Besides, I have other work in the Congo."

Maybe it was the dark plane cabin and the droning fuselage, or the collective lull of so many sleeping bodies, but in the overlapping halos of our reading lights, I felt as if we were alone.

"You're also an anthropologist?" I asked as she put away her phone.

"Among the many things I've been, yes, that's one of them."

Her words made me realize that society had trained me to expect statements of career change and exploration from men. I wanted to ask if and where she'd studied anthropology, but I sensed her reticence, possibly a desire not to be pigeonholed, and this further lit up my brain.

"What are you doing in the Congo?" she asked.

I smiled, suddenly uneasy, trying to hear my answer before I spoke it.

"I'm a journalist. I'm working on a story about, well, an American who has been living in the rainforest for three decades, who's basically gone rogue."

"A Kurtz?" she said and laughed.

"Yes," I admitted, feeling less self-conscious. "I wish it were otherwise."

"Well, if you don't find him, I'm sure you'll stumble across some other ones."

"That's the backup plan."

"Are you independent?"

"I am. It leaves time for personal writing. Years ago, when I began doing this, I'd buy a one-way ticket to strand myself overseas and then write to make enough money to pay my way back. It taught me to find stories everywhere."

"It sounds as if you could have become a Kurtz yourself."

"It wasn't inconceivable."

Coming down the aisle sideways, an old white man in khaki clutched the seats. He encroached on our circle of light like a night creature testing a boundary—and then loomed over us, before lurching on.

She reached up to the reading lights and turned one off.

I considered what to say next, refraining from asking a question that would tie her coloring to Africa or mark her interest there as part of her heritage. But she spoke first, the absence of any strong regional inflection in her voice again making me wonder if English wasn't her native language.

"I suppose you might like to write about our little white witch."

"I would of course credit the anthropologist's work and interview him."

"That should do the job." She laughed. "He is no enemy to recognition."

The story of a black girl possessed by a white demon and turned white was already lacerating the edges of my imagination, and I was glad for her response.

She talked more about the girl, about how the anthropologist had been interviewing her with the help of a Congolese interpreter before transcribing and then translating her responses.

"His project is fraught. He asks questions in French that the interpreter translates to Lingala, since the girl doesn't respond to French, despite her rudimentary grasp. The translator then renders her answers into French, from which my friend translates them into English, since he is doing post-doctoral work at Dartmouth. We must assume that a lot is lost."

I liked how she spoke—the fluency of her pauses, as if she were simply emphasizing, and how, sometimes, she turned her palms up to stress a point, loosely knitting her fingers.

Past her shoulder, the night topography began to shift, and she followed my gaze. She tapped the button on the window, clearing the dark tint from the glass, and we were suddenly staring down at an alien horizon of bottom-lit clouds, as if flying over a gas giant. The alienating distance from our planet registered in my body, a pulse of uncertainty in the nerves along the bones of my chest.

"So how did you get into writing?" she asked, suddenly sounding tired.

"I grew up poor, and we didn't have much in the house other than used books my mom picked up. She had artistic ambitions for me, to say the least, and there wasn't much else to do but read or go to the library."

I suddenly felt divided. I wanted to say, "Stories saved my life." It was a line I often found myself thinking, during moments when I considered what a truly narrative species we are—measured, constrained, or liberated by story. I sometimes said it when giving talks, since it jolted the audience into presence, into a connection with me. It was exaggerated in a way that obliged people to listen closely, to judge whether I was being authentic, and in that moment I could offer the best I had.

I glanced past her, to where the moon peered at us from above the plunging curve of the earth, beneath the cavernous hood of space. I hesitated, afraid of being manipulative, but that we were among the few passengers not overcome by torpor gave me a sense of being separate, even special—or at least of intimacy and trust.

"Stories," I said, "novels, actually—they saved my life."

She turned a little more toward me and looked into my eyes, waiting.

"My father had a fifth-grade education," I told her. "When he saw me reading, he would hunch and glare at me. I guess my reading must have made him feel smaller, like a failure. He'd never read a novel, and I often read one a day.

"Anyway, he told me how the future should look, but I knew there were other futures. I'd read them in books."

The sunrise emanated from the clouds, shining on the wingtip like a star and creeping red along the metal. The hum of the fuselage had become faintly shrill, and our fatigue was suddenly apparent. The air felt staticky as she yawned. There were circles under her eyes.

"I'm sorry," she said and touched my wrist. "Thank you for sharing that."

"The fatigue comes on hard, doesn't it?"

"It's as if we see the sun and realize we haven't really slept."

I wanted to finish the story, but it seemed too much to explain my eroding faith in free will, or that novels had also taught me to chase impossibilities, conjuring villains as I crossed the planet to find them.

I was again tempted to ask where she was from—to cement her in my mind as a person I knew so I could quell my sudden feeling of vulnerability, even though I often divulged my story in lecture halls. But I refused to speak the question that she no doubt heard more often than any other. Rather, I wished I could delete not only that impulse from my brain but also my memories of the culture that had created it.

She was turned away, facing the window, and the light fractured around her, cut by her curling strands of hair and the line of her neck.

All along the blazing wing, the sunrise bled.

2

PASTOR THOMAS OMÉGA

In the minutes before landing, I fell into a dream. Descending a stairwell, I came upon my father sitting, stroking a big calico cat that lazed on his lap.

The wheels bumped the runway, and I woke. The antimalarial I'd taken, Pentus, was new on the market, and I'd read that it could induce Technicolor dreams or visions but that the effect mellowed in the days after each weekly dose.

Sola looked at me quizzically, maybe shyly, as I stood up to take down my backpack. I must have appeared groggy and tried to smile. I gave her my card, and she said she would e-mail me. Then we were corralled off the plane while saying goodbye, which proved unnecessary, as we ended up walking through the airport and having breakfast together.

By the time we boarded our connection, she'd given me her e-mail and Congo number, and though I briefly considered finding a way to sit with her, I'd booked today's flight for a reason and had work to do. She was seated not far behind me, in the company of a tall man with a handsome profile who struck up a conversation, smiling and gesticulating, and I noticed that three rows ahead of me, the seat next to Pastor Thomas Oméga was empty. He hadn't appeared to have noticed me, even though we'd spoken at a conference a week before and he'd told me which day he would be flying back to the Congo. He'd encouraged me to take the same flight so he could facilitate my investigation into the practices of conservation organizations—which was how I'd presented my work, not mentioning the individual who was my focus.

As the fuselage resonated with the thud of the closing cabin door, I stood, stepped quickly up the aisle, and sat.

"Ah," he said, "je savais que tu allais me trouver"—I knew you would find me.

Round was the word that came to mind each time I saw him. He wasn't fat at all but possessed a defining roundness that seemed almost muscular; it was apparent in his face and carriage, and in the accentuation of his cheekbones as he smiled. An older white woman sat to his right, engrossed in *Le Monde*, and I was looking forward to hours of his undivided attention.

"So how was the conference?" I asked in French.

"The usual," he said and laughed with pleasure, as if the usual were remarkable. "Everyone was making bigger and bigger promises and declaring all we would accomplish together, so that by the time it was over, we left feeling that we had made peace in Africa and saved its forests and animals."

"Sounds like a conference," I said.

"Yes. The food was delicious. And the young women environmentalists are so in love with Africans that it was hard to say no."

"But of course you did." I elbowed him and he laughed again.

"Do you know that this was my first time in America? It was better than I expected, though stressful. For years, I have read the news online, and every day a Jean-Pierre Bemba is shooting up malls, cinemas, and schools. But I survived!"

He wore a pastel blue shirt with large mother-of-pearl buttons, and he touched one at his throat, tracing a fingertip over its surface.

"I also went to Chicago to raise money for a new church, since my congregation is growing. While I was there, a pastor took me to see the door of the Church of Satan. No such thing could exist in the Congo. The people would rise up. We would burn it. We wouldn't accept that evil exist so openly."

He was looking at me expectantly, and I said, "I think most Americans don't really believe in that stuff, so we just ignore it."

"But some Americans believe in it enough to build satanic churches."

"I suppose, but they aren't common."

"You sound like a man who hasn't experienced the spirit of God speaking through him, so maybe you simply cannot see the invisible power of evil as I can."

I was tempted to say something about visible evil—the corrupt elite who ran Kinshasa, who let their countrymen starve while liquidating the Congo's minerals to Europe, China, and America. I wanted to ask why people didn't rise up and destroy them. But he was tight with that crowd and besides, religion had always distracted people from real evil. Though I needed to steer the conversation back to the conference, I feared appearing opportunistic. So I told him about the girl and the white demon, considering that his insights might nourish what I wrote about her.

He listened intently and said, "Yes, this is a problem in the Congo. There are many street children. It used to be that the only witches were old people. You knew they were sorcerers from their ancient faces and stayed far enough away that their demons couldn't jump into you. But when the demons got the idea of hiding in children, many people were infected, since children are hard to avoid."

"But aren't they just children that nobody wants?"

His look became wary in a way I knew from my years overseas: he was deciding whether to explain a belief that I was certain to discount.

"Yes," he said, "most of them aren't demons. They're from poor families, and a stepmother or stepfather accuses them so that there will be one fewer mouth to feed. But sometimes there are children inhabited by demons. I'm a pastor. I've done this work. The demon will speak through the child to name the people it has killed."

"Isn't it likely that the children have come to believe in superstition?"

"Absolutely not. It is real. You will see. I will take you to see."

"But maybe the child is sick in some way or mentally ill . . ."

"I have seen them cough up human flesh. I have seen the demon rise out of them when they are cured. You *mundele* like your science. You explain how disease works, its mechanisms, and of course it's all true, but you cannot explain why."

"Why someone gets sick?"

"Why *that* person gets sick in *that* moment. This is the work of a spirit. Yes, we all know about bacteria and viruses. But the spirit is what causes them to affect one person and not the other. It is the reason that we watch. A demon enters a family and money is lost. A demon goes into a business or military unit, and people turn against each other."

"I would call such things misfortune or just natural conflict."

"What would be the point of God creating a world where chance rules? Do you not pray?"

"Personally, no, but—"

"Have you never looked to the sky and asked why, or closed your eyes and demanded that the world be different—begged for it to be different?"

The woman to Oméga's right ruffled the pages of her newspaper, conveying disapproval at the rising tenor of our discussion, and I lowered my voice.

"I guess there are moments in my life when I've involuntarily done that."

"So there," he said and laughed.

My fatigue was palpable, my legs leaden, and my ears rang with the reverb of strained nerves. My mind seemed to withdraw far behind my skull. The man across the aisle slumped forward, a magazine in his lap and his bald crown against the seatback in front of him.

"I was actually hoping to talk about Richmond Hew," I told Oméga.

His posture became alert. "What business do you have with him?" he asked in a tense, quiet voice.

"I'm working on an exposé. I've heard that you're not a fan."

I instantly realized my mistake. This knowledge revealed that I'd known far more about Oméga than I'd let on at the conference—that someone else had fed me information about both him and Hew.

Without turning, he looked at me with an oblique movement of his eyes.

"All changes need to be made gently," he said, his tone now more measured.

I'd taken his gregariousness to be a sign of trust and future complicity—a mistake I'd previously made in the Congo. By speaking so soon about what I wanted, I might actually have revealed my lack of judgment and discipline. Such missteps were generally forgiven in foreigners, though they caused unease.

"From the perspective of many American donors, Hew"—he pronounced his name *Eww* in French—"is a hero, even if they almost never speak of him in public."

I cleared my throat and sipped from the water bottle I'd tucked into the seatback pouch. I took stock of what I could say without further betraying to Oméga how well I'd researched him—that I knew of his likely ministerial appointment.

"Hew has a colonial attitude," I said. "He's in the tradition of Leopold and Stanley. Sure, he's made national parks and protected endangered species, but he's done it for himself, so he can rule the rainforest like a king."

Oméga still faced ahead, still watched me askance, his brow hiked with skepticism above the round eye he'd charged with evaluating me. I felt that I'd largely recovered my fumble, and though my references to colonial figures were heavy-handed, there was a tradition in the Congo of leveling such comparisons.

"I will consider this," he said. "I haven't been in politics recently. President Kabila is like his father in some ways, in others not. I have nostalgia for the early days of the war when all seemed possible. But they have passed, and God has called me. If He tells me to return to politics, or even to war, I will do it. I am his servant."

3

LITERATURE CONNECTS US TO THE EARTH

When we landed, the sun was a smoldering meteor, already plummeting toward the horizon, the way it did in the lower latitudes.

At immigrations, as Oméga and I spoke, the white woman stood behind us and, having folded *Le Monde* into her purse, sighed impatiently. He went ahead, a roundness in how he walked, the fullness of presence or authority, as if he inhabited an orb that moved through space. He passed quickly, and I followed. In the baggage claim, I wondered if he would distance himself, but he waved me over. We stood at the conveyor belt, talking as coffin-sized packages wrapped in cellophane rode past.

Sola came into the room, walked up to us, and shook Oméga's hand.

"Pastor Thomas Oméga." He dipped his head.

"Sola," she said. She couldn't have been much older than her early thirties. She was of medium height, but with her poise and direct gaze, she had the sort of presence that made me think of spiritual and mental training, or perhaps concerted healing from trauma.

Oméga said a few words in Lingala, and she responded haltingly before they shifted to French—a language that she spoke fluently despite her slight accent, which had suddenly revealed itself more clearly.

"You are American?" he asked.

"I am," she replied, and the pause that followed was brief—a terse silence.

"You're here for work?"

"Yes. And you? Is this home or a visit?"

"Home," he said, "though sometimes I wonder what that really means."

She'd been observing him but now her eyes became more alert, lifting slightly to search into his. Though he hadn't posed a direct question as I might have, his contemplative statement had quietly invited her to share her pedigree.

A gray, hard-bodied roller bag passed on the conveyor, and she caught it.

"It's been a pleasure meeting you," she told him and then smiled at me. She neared her hand to her cheek, signaling that she would call, before striding to the exit, beyond which someone was waiting for her—a thin, gaunt man in a pale suit motioning from the crowd seconds after the door swished open.

Oméga also watched her go.

"What leads to a man meeting a beautiful woman on a flight?" he asked. "You can say chance, but if that's so, then how drab life is. I say the spirits or God's design. Then we have a world that is fully alive."

I caught myself midshrug and tried to make myself appear less dismissive.

"I think the design is in the story," I replied.

"How so?"

"A man who is happily married might sit next to an attractive woman, and she will not fit into the story he tells himself about his life. But for a single man, especially the eternally single type, the opposite may be true."

"Yes, but we must separate man's illusions from the divine order."

"Maybe the divine order is simply our grandest illusion. I know many people who believe that everything that happens is fated. They meet their spouses and say it was meant to be, but a few years later they divorce."

Oméga laughed. "And then the story becomes one of trials and growth."

He stepped away to pull a bulging suitcase off the conveyor belt, and then a second and a third.

"Come," he told me. "I'll drop you off at your hotel."

Not long after, a bodyguard, it seemed—given the man's girth and carriage—arrived with the driver and helped load Oméga's luggage into a new, powerfully air-conditioned Land Rover. The two men sat in front, Oméga and I behind them, and we drove into the city, past Armageddon scenes of roadside fires and people running through the headlights of charging traffic. Their sudden silhouettes—impressions of fragility and endurance—stung my retina, awakening memories of a worse time, when I'd last been here, during the war.

"How did you become a journalist?" Oméga asked, his voice now muted with fatigue. "A family connection or a desire for justice?"

"Actually," I told him, "I intended to be a novelist."

"A novelist?" he repeated.

"Yes, I loved books as a child and . . . and, in a sense, I guess they saved me."

I hesitated, but Oméga seemed genuinely interested.

"My family was poor," I continued, "and novels gave me the impression of infinite possibility. As a child, I often read novels of gifted, solitary youths desperate to escape a repressive rural place. For them, saving the world was an excuse to set out and discover it, and be transformed. Years ago, I was hired as a research guide for a rich university student with internationalist ambitions and I took him to Nairobi. 'Isn't this amazing?' I kept saying, but he'd already seen it all on YouTube. He experienced it as information, not as a sanctuary from his past or a gateway to a new self."

Maybe exhaustion was releasing the thoughts my conversation with Sola had stirred up. My words came out more intimate than I intended: how stories deepened my love of landscape, connecting me to the world in a way that I still experience only when I'm in motion.

My grandmother once told me that loquacity ran in the family, an impulse so strong it had to be a biological mandate. So I let myself finish, saying that the young man of the YouTube generation hadn't first encountered distant places as the reward for bodily exertion. He hadn't experienced them as reveries merging into sight, becoming memory before they'd been fully felt in the nerves of the eyes.

Oméga sat in silence, perhaps waiting to be sure that I'd completed my thoughts, before he spoke in an enlivened voice.

"Books were the same for me, and freedom is why many of us came to Kinshasa." He gestured to the driver and bodyguard, and they nodded. "We also wanted a future. Even my name, Oméga, is taken from a poem. I was a young man. This was during the war in the east, when I often faced death. I came into a house that had been pillaged. A book was on the floor. It was the poems of Arthur Rimbaud, and I read 'Vowels,' in which each letter has a color and an image:

Silences crossed by Worlds and Angels:
— O the Omega, the violet ray of His Eyes!

I decided then that I would survive and preach God's word, that I would take the name Oméga. I could sense the violet light pouring out of His loving eyes."

I myself had read this poem as a teenager, wishing I had synesthesia, but my response now seemed impoverished by the vitality of Oméga's. I felt guilty that, while speaking, I'd worried that the cultural context of everything I was sharing would be too removed. I'd skimmed, saying nothing of agency and purpose—villains and the intensity of solitude in foreign lands.

"The Bible," Oméga pressed on, "was of course the most important book for me. There were nights in the war when I lay in my shelter recalling the stories in Kings and Prophets. The machine guns fired and the mortars fell and I was Elijah listening for the word of God in the thunder and trembling earth."

The Land Rover had turned onto a narrow road, past a car's stripped-down carcass in the ditch, in a nest of weeds that had grown through and around it.

"I'm glad you shared your story," he said. "Normally, I don't like foreign journalists. Their investigations begin with a judgment, and they have come to find the evidence of what they already believe. But you are welcome in my church and home. You will have dinner with my wife and daughters. How do you like the sound of that?"

"That sounds quite nice."

"Quite nice? Ha! You *mundele* speak pearly words but are all jackals."

He turned in the seat next to me. In the street light, his fingers were again on the button of his shirt. They shifted to his collar, holding it, and then peeled it back.

A thick, glossy scar twisted from the base of his throat, near his jugular, and ran down toward his heart.

"And then I will tell you the story of my scar, and you will know why my congregation calls me *prophète.* Maybe you will begin to see. I've read about the brain and how our beliefs can keep us from seeing the truth. Maybe in the Congo you will learn that there are powers you don't understand, and you'll realize why books have saved you. All books are leading us back to the one good book."

4

ROOM 22(2)
&
THE WILDLIFE OF ASPEN

At the hotel, I was so stunned when the clerk handed me my room card that I failed to ask for a different one before he moved on to the next guest. I took the elevator up and walked directly to the door. Two metal squares read 22 next to a patch of adhesive where the third had hung. I swiped and stepped inside, and stood in the gloom of drawn blinds outlined by the city's faint electric effusion.

Room 22(2) had been my home for five months during my trip here over a decade ago, when I decided to become a war reporter. In the French style, the second floor was two stories up from the ground level—"too high to jump and yet too close to the violence in the streets to feel safe," I joked with friends. The nation was Zaire back then, for a few weeks after my arrival, before Laurent-Désiré Kabila marched out of the east and into Kinshasa with a ragtag army of Congolese and battle-hardened Rwandan Tutsis, set up his government in the hotel's top floors, and rolled back the country's name to Congo.

Evenings, when I went downstairs to see what was on the menu, men with gold glasses, bejeweled rings, and suits more expensive than everything I owned combined sometimes invited me to their tables. For lack of an Eastern European weapons dealer, they had me sit with them. "*Un journaliste*," they said and laughed. "You've come to the Congo at the right time, my friend." Other evenings, they left me alone, as they were already seated with more authentic figures—white men with narrow faces, crooked, tightly shaved jaws, and gazes that were cold, unwavering, and predatory.

In my room, I awakened each sunrise to an avocado on my windowsill. I'd received it one afternoon, during a long power outage when I was trying to finish an article before my laptop battery died. Someone had banged on the door, and when I opened it, a paratrooperish man exuding the etheric cloud of prolonged inebriation said he'd knocked on the wrong one but then, in a low voice, warned me not to write offensive nonsense, before peeling the hand grenade off his vest with an extravagant gesture of bounty—as if he were the tree of life—and handing it to me.

"You never know," he told me and laughed, showing a broken tooth.

A few months later, the embers of the First Congo War—which had rippled out from the Rwandan Genocide—reignited in the east, fracturing the country and precipitating the Second Congo War: a continuation of one long bloodletting in the eyes of many Congolese. As its massacres began, I left the hotel to get a closer look at a despairing people, to interview warlords, the hollow-faced human rights activists and UN inspectors tasked with body counts, and the *mai-mai* militiamen doused in the holy oils that made both them and their enemies believe they were bulletproof.

In the years since the Congo wars, I worked in Afghanistan, Somalia, Colombia, and Iraq before moving to Brooklyn, where I fell into a slump, not answering messages, lying in bed all day reading and leaving my sublet only for groceries.

One night, a friend passing through the city convinced me to meet her for dinner with the promise of a journalistic scoop. She told me that the US had allocated millions to protect the Congo rainforest and that corporate conservation organizations, the majority of which had failed to get a foothold there during both Mobutu's dictatorship and the war, had, in the decade since, been jockeying for the areas of highest biodiversity, often doing harm to local social structures and wasting as many resources competing with each other as they used for conservation.

The timing was fortuitous, since I was living off credit cards. The next day, I e-mailed a pitch to *Mother Jones*—"Big Conservation's Scramble for Africa"—and a week later, I flew to Aspen, Colorado, for a conference that was bringing together organizations and donors to discuss the Congo's future.

The lodge where I'd booked a room—the cheapest I could find—had an unpainted wood exterior and interior that gave it a look less rustic than outmoded. A stout woman with a yellow perm checked me in and then put a placemat-sized map in front of me.

"You can walk along the river here," she told me, sliding her finger along a blue line. "It's a nice trail, though sometimes people run into mountain lions on it. But if you're looking for cougars, I would suggest these three bars near the lifts."

"Pardon me," I said. "I'm not sure I understand."

"Come on. You're a handsome young man who's checked in alone, and most of the guys who come here try out the cougar bars. Aspen has some of the richest cougars in the country—the ex-trophy wives of millionaires and billionaires." She made a vague motion to her face and chest. "Which means the best doctors and the hottest cougars."

I thanked her, and after a light dinner at a nearby restaurant, I went for a jog along the fragrant hedges of high-summer Aspen. On all sides, summits curtailed the night sky, cradling the few, vivid stars. The purity and thinness of the mountain air made the insides of my lungs feel pleasantly scraped. There was a slight altitude-induced tightness at the back of my neck, and a stinging each time I took a breath, but though I was tired, when I returned to my bed, I couldn't sleep.

I got up and dressed without the light, since I hoped the dark might lull me back to bed, but my brain glowed with the thought of a previously unimagined romantic connection after so many months without even going on a date—and then I was unplugging my phone and stepping out.

The bar was an elegant fusion of oaken frontier virtue and classic speakeasy leather, though the only thing smoky about the place was its lack of visibility. The designer must have specialized in lighting for a certain kind of face. The ambience was dusky and smoothing, like a social media filter for everything after midlife.

There were no mirrors. Draped and veiled in fashionable shadows, the women were each other's mirrors. And yet the eye needs a fraction of a second to judge an artificial smile. Real ones fluctuate, hesitate, an entire language in how they linger. These were fairy tale smiles, waiting beneath ice.

At the table nearest me, a woman's pale-violet gown cleaved to precise curves, and she turned, advertising a countenance as smooth as a plaque.

Another woman, this one my age and with blond dreads like hawsers, sat across from her.

"Looking for someone?" she asked.

"I'm in town for a conference. I thought I'd have a drink before bed."

She slapped the seat next to her. "Join us. I'm here for it too."

The older woman moved her lips faintly, some disappointment showing in her eyes, and then stood and crossed the bar.

"She's saying hi to a friend," the dreadlocked woman told me. "Oh, I'm Terra."

"Terra Sylvan-Gaia?"

"Shit. My reputation precedes me."

"I've read about your work," I said but refrained from adding that I'd expected someone closer to Jane Goodall and Dian Fossey's generation. It was too soon to discuss my research, so I made small talk, asking how much time she'd spent in Aspen.

"A fair bit. My aunt lives here. I've been catching up with her." She lifted her jaw in the direction of the woman who'd left the table.

Terra must have read something in my expression, since she added, "Cougars run in the family, but that's because beauty and money do, though never enough. It's hard to give up any sort of power, and since beautiful women are weak on shelf life and those in my family are smart enough to know it, we're strong on prenuptials."

I felt slightly taken aback, uninformed and parochial in comparison to her matter-of-fact assessment of the scene around us: the young men arriving alone in jeans and tight T-shirts, flaunting gym-fit biceps, and soon downing the single malt whiskeys that their straight-backed dames ordered with a regal lift of a finger.

I did my best to hide my discomfort, since Terra was one of the people I hoped to interview. I'd learned about her from articles—though not when she'd confectioned her name or who she'd been before—and I was uncertain as to her allegiance with the big organizations that were carving the Congo into fiefdoms. I knew only that she lived among a rare gorilla species, a largely forgotten cousin to the famed mountain gorilla, in the war-torn east.

As we got to talking about her work and its ever-elusive funding, she made it instantly clear—"off the record," she said, when I told her I was a journalist—that she was no friend to the big organizations. She was here in a last-ditch effort to win over a certain former four-star general and possible future presidential candidate who would be in attendance, since he was a major donor and adviser to nature foundations.

She then began talking about working overseas and the ravages of being eternally single.

"Men like the idea of me," she said.

"I know exactly what you mean, but with women."

She studied my face for a moment.

"You don't seem like a journalist to me."

"Why's that?"

"Too thoughtful. There's too much emotion under the surface. You're a cogitator if I've ever seen one—a Pisces, I bet . . ."

I hated astrology and mystical quackery, and was considering how to respond when she asked, "What drives you?"

"I guess . . . I guess it's a manic sense of responsibility, the idea that—"

"I knew it," she said. "We're the casualties of a generation of bleeding heart liberal parents."

She wasn't wrong, and I told her how my mother had raised me to be aware of every injustice (racism, imperialism, the war on drugs, the death penalty, nuclear armament, the abuses of crony capitalism).

"Are you on medication?" she asked.

"No, but I do microdose with lithium," I confessed, "though that's a mineral. Really, it should be in all multivitamins."

"Is it prescribed?"

"I get it on Amazon. I read an article about it in the *New York Times*."

"And it works?"

"It's hard to say. I started it at the same time as vitamin D megadoses."

"Vitamin D is fucking manna. Every person in America should be mainlining it!"

I nodded, blanking briefly as I wondered what her standards for a thoughtful man were, but then she realized that I hadn't mentioned my name. I told her and she said, "Béchard? Is that French Canadian?"

"Yes," I said. "I'm half."

"Oh. What a tease. I wish I were free. *J'aime les Québécois*.

They're so earthy, so bodily. My family used to go on summer vacations up there. We had a little beach place in the Gaspé, on the water. My father would tell me how much he loved the peasant exuberance of the French Canadians and the joie de vivre despite the poverty. He always talked about those dark French Canadian beauties. He was a total pig beneath his WASP trappings, but I loved him. Anyway, I was up in *Montréal* for a conference recently, and, man, *c'était le fun!* I really hope your American side hasn't screwed you up."

"I hope not too," I said, not sure if I should be offended or flattered, and certain that I'd been screwed up from all sides: collaboration on a grand scale.

Maybe she sensed my discomfort or lack of words, because she circled back to the subject of responsibility. I was feeling guarded now, exposed when I was supposed to be the one doing the exposé, and I wanted to reinvest myself with journalistic restraint. So I listened to her talk about her drive to do something for the world, the innocence and kindness of gorillas, their purity, and how protecting them alleviated her perpetual sense of guilt.

I sympathized. Sometimes, like tonight, by going to a cougar bar, I did things to defy my sense of moral obligation—though also to step out of my life, into a circumstance where my self might become so unfamiliar that I could briefly perceive it.

Terra stood and picked up her corduroy jacket and purse.

"Normally," she said, "I'd invite you back to my hotel, but I'm saving my eligibility for the general. It would be weird to disengage tomorrow so that I can seduce him."

"I can see how that could be problematic," I replied.

As soon as she left, her aunt, Michaela, returned and sat

with me. The stillness of her face made it appear carefully balanced as it tilted toward me on her long neck. She'd been a choreographer and was now an art collector. She spoke softly, intelligently. We forget how much we hear words simply from facial expressions. I moved closer, inclining my ear toward her, and we remained like that, in murmured conversation, until the bar closed, and we said good night.

The next day, I switched to the hotel hosting the conference to take advantage of the attendee rate. The inaugural event was just starting, and the hall seemed to proclaim nature's salvation, its windows built to frame the views and catch the refracted softness of mountain light.

Everyone was murmuring about the general, and when the lean, gray-haired man entered, Terra was already at his side, her dreadlocks hidden in a white turban that made the blues and whites of her eyes shine in her tanned face. She displayed her freckled cleavage in a long green dress, as if nature had cleverly sent a white dryad to steer the general toward the deliverance of black people's forests.

He took the stage and in the gruff voice of leadership, worldliness, and pragmatism painted the future of conservation with a watery mix of magniloquence and corporate euphemism. The twenty-minute talk boiled down to saving the rainforests and their species, which he compared to renaissance art, from the hoi polloi who want to cut down or fry up everything, but how, alas, the saving could be done only with the help of the hoi polloi, by educating them, by brotherhood, etc.

Terra was waiting as he descended, and with his sylph at his side, he took questions, the crowd turning around them—a great Charybdis of networking. Eventually, conferees broke into groups that, from their postures, suggested the animals they hoped to protect: a sloth, a skulk, a bloat at the buffet; a troop and pandemonium at the wine bar; a bask, a rout, a zeal, all near the high windows, admiring a pink sunset.

As I loitered, the talk seemed perfunctory—who was on the ground, doing what. The conferees spoke in appropriated oppression (slaving away at a project, shackled to their desks) but as soon as they learned I was a journalist, they became wary or excused themselves.

One man wandered between flock and busyness with an air of exile. As if he'd acquired a skin irritation in some tropical redoubt, or simply a mosquito bite, he kept scratching his back, going about with his elbow lifted like a dorsal fin.

I intercepted him. His eyes were brown—soft, intelligent, a little shut down, as if he expected to be made fun of.

"A journalist!" he said. "I shouldn't be seen talking to you, but I shouldn't even be here. I booked this conference the week before I was laid off. Funding cuts. The eternal funding cuts that target the dissenters."

I knew I'd found my man and barely had to prompt.

"Nature conservation is bullshit," he told me. "The reality is we're consigned to offices and our relationship to the field is that of excursionists on weekend outings. I'm serious. We're disconnected. That's why people can't out someone like you—"

"Pardon me?"

"Someone like Hew," he repeated in a whisper, though hundreds of voices clamored in the hall. "H-E-W. It's the name no one's saying but everyone's thinking."

"I haven't heard of him."

"He's the node in the jungle they plug their machine

into. Without him, the lights don't turn on. No grand successes to brag about. No pretty maps of new parkland. No photos of dashing white men in khaki with smiling Pygmies. That's what this conference is really about—the illusion of achievement in order to raise money. Terra is surrounded by enemies. She's trying to save herself from Hew."

"I'm sorry. I don't understand."

"What you need to get is that the real cannibals in the jungle are the big Western organizations. They chase donor cash, and those who get it consume the projects of those who don't. Everyone here is a competitor, but they're forced to put on good faces and spout salvationist doctrine. Now, Terra, she's the real deal. It's her work that's about to be devoured. She used to be a typical tree hugger—"

"Aren't all conservationists tree huggers?"

"Hardly. We live and breathe realpolitik. It's like believing in democracy and human rights but having to do business with China."

"Or other countries believing in democracy and human rights but having to do business with the US."

"Point taken. Anyway, Terra is a little on the crunchy woo-woo mystical side of things, but she does phenomenal work. She goes native at quantum speeds. Believes in their values. Participates in their ceremonies. Holds and kisses the babies. None of it's for show. She's been living out there for a decade, trying to generate support for the eastern lowland gorilla, but it never caught on as a species. It had a bad name and wasn't sexy. It lacked the primal, hippie shagginess of the mountain gorillas."

He was animated now, rubbing his knuckles against his palm, as if to purée the information he was conveying, afraid I'd fail to digest it.

"Now imagine this. The big organizations don't want to support her because her style of conservation is all local initiative and doesn't show up on the map in the form of parks, which the big organizations need to brag about to raise money. That's when Hew gets involved. Richmond Hew. Look him up. He's been in the Congo thirty years, even during the war. He knows the gears of power and if the big organizations fill his coffers, he'll come in like a conqueror, throw around a lot of cash, get locals to sign conservation agreements, and then kick them off the land. He'll destroy everything she's built."

Other attendees were glancing over at us now, a few gesturing with concern.

"Just talking to you like this," he said and blinked a few times, nervously, as if to calm a facial spasm, "it's going to ruin me. Conservation is the mafia. I'll never work again. But fuck it—this is my conscience speaking. I got into the game for good reasons, and it has poisoned me. So this is the last thing I'll tell you. Hew is dangerous. I mean, really, really dangerous. People gossip about him. Fucked up stories make their way out. Murder. Rape. Some stuff to do with little girls. But we keep throwing money at him."

"Would you be willing to go on the record with any of this?" I asked.

"No. I don't know. Maybe. Tell me your name. I'll find you online."

As soon as I handed him my card, he hurried off, in the direction of the bathrooms, and I drifted from gaggle to parade—from ambush to leap to charm—without luck. Then the buffet was carted off and the hall emptied, and the building was silent but for the distant hard shoes of a staff person closing up for the night.

A few hours later, after a long session researching Hew and gorillas online, I headed to the hotel spa to use the sauna.

The hallway was softly lit, creating a nocturnal ambiance, and in the distance I recognized Terra, walking barefoot along the tan carpet, her dress disheveled and her dreadlocks loose.

"How's the general?" I asked.

"He took an Ambien, I did a line. We had fun, but we weren't in the same groove. I'll reclaim him in the morning."

As she sighed, her bloodshot eyes looked me up and down, as if inspecting a freshly painted post.

"How's the prospecting going?" she asked.

"Not bad. I was actually wondering if you would talk to me about Richmond Hew."

"Of course I'll talk to you about Hew." She lifted her arm as if declaring her words on stage. "Anything you want to know. Gun running. Diamond smuggling. He's tied up in everything. The guy is a warlord. He's about to ruin my fucking life. The Congolese love me and they tell me his secrets. He fucks little girls. He's murdered people. He'll do anything to stay in power. You should talk to Thomas Oméga tomorrow. He's the pastor of the Congo's president and he's here. Rumors have it he's next in line for a sinecure as the minister of the environment."

She was wearing a small pouch on a string around her neck and dipped her fingers into it.

"Here," she said, "chew this."

The dried leaves crackled in my mouth. They were spicy. My lips and tongue felt as if they were buzzing. I had the impression that my face was one of those surrealist portraits of a face composed of other objects, flowers or vegetables—in my case, bees.

“What is that?” I asked.

“Something the gorillas love. I call it ‘gorilla love.’”

My throat was beginning to itch, and I considered asking if she had an EpiPen but didn’t want to come across as dramatic. The tingling spread down along my neck and chest, and suddenly I had an erection.

I was afraid that she would notice, but a look of exhaustion had come over her. Her high was ending and she was crashing. She took a few heavy steps to an upholstered bench in a recess, and sat.

“Are you okay?” I asked, the itching in my throat increasingly manageable.

“I’m great,” she said and smiled. She placed her hand on her knee and slid it along the inside of her thigh, drawing back her dress and showing white panties.

Then she closed her eyes and her head dropped back against the wall, and she was asleep.

I turned hesitantly and, hobbling ever so slightly, made my way to my suite.

Two weeks later, by the time I stepped into the familiarity of room 22(2), Oméga was my lone contact, since the embittered conservationist had failed to write, and, a few days after Aspen, Terra had returned to her site in the eastern Congo only to vanish on a dirt road near Butembo. Her 4Runner was found overturned in a ditch, riddled by bullets, and she, her supplies, and her driver were gone.

5

MEMOIRS OF THE LITTLE WITCH

I stood on a vast, misted river, staring for the far, dim shore with a longing as palpable as a bruised organ. Then a siren rang out and the dream vaporized to the electric blatting of the telephone. It sounded like a phaser in an old sci-fi flick.

The grenade was absent on the windowsill, and I now saw how different the room was—all the modernization I'd failed to notice upon my jetlagged arrival.

I coughed and cleared my throat, said, "Oui, bonjour," into my shoulder as a test run to make sure my vocal cords worked, and then snatched the receiver.

"C'est moi," a woman said—Sola, I realized, and was fully awake. "I'm heading over to meet the anthropologist and the girl. Would you like to join?"

"Yes. Of course," I replied, pestered by my relief that she had yet to see him. She told me which neighborhood she'd stayed in and where the anthropologist lived, and we calculated that she was coming from a different direction. Picking me up would add an hour to her trip in Kinshasa traffic, so I said I'd take a taxi.

"If you get there first," she told me, "please wait. It would be best if I introduce you."

On the drive, I realized that I'd forgotten how difficult it was to hold Kinshasa in my mind—to see it fully. So much was constantly happening on all sides that, even as I stared out the taxi window, the city came only in glimpses: people talking, vending, bartering, arguing, relaxing, sleeping on the roadside, eating at tiny stands beneath patched beer umbrellas, or running through traffic.

The building I arrived at was a single story of concrete, with the drabness of a storehouse but not the height, the starkness of a public school but too few windows and doors. Only when my entrance interrupted Sola's argument with the anthropologist, and I heard its subject, did I decide the ambience was that of a jail.

Bram Rees was dapper, with leather half boots, ironed khakis, a white linen shirt, and a blue bandana knotted at his throat. I checked my impulse to judge, since, had I the same boyish face, I might also have indulged in a little sartorial character building. He was a redhead, sprucely coiffed, but with large Raggedy Ann freckles so tightly clustered on each cheek they looked, from a distance, like a circle of rouge, such as you might expect on a porcelain doll.

"One second," Sola told me when I came in the door, holding up a finger in my direction while still facing him. She was flushed, her curly hair loose, and she wore jeans and a black long-sleeved shirt.

"Sola," Bram said, "can we not bring this up in front of our guest? He is after all"—and here his voice sounded like a stage whisper—"a journalist." He opened his eyes wide in an expression I suspected had been with us since our simian days: a way of saying danger.

"She was—is—a child," Sola told him, "not a test subject."

"I don't see your point. Plenty of children are test subjects."

"You locked her up. You locked up a child, like a prisoner."

"She was insane. *Is* insane. She had a demon in her. She pointed her finger at me like this." He shaped his hand into a gun and flicked his thumb to show the hammer coming down.

"Of course she did. You had her locked up. You didn't earn her trust."

Bram dodged Sola, took a long step toward me as if lunging with a rapier, and clasped my hand in both of his. His fragile, sun-distressed skin revealed anxiety and the many fine wrinkles that would soon bestow upon him the gravitas he craved.

"It's such a pleasure to meet you," he said. "Welcome, welcome. Sola told me that you might be interested in my rather challenging work."

The story I gradually composed from their argument and Bram's flustered explanations was that a police officer he'd tipped off to look for street children accused of sorcery—his subject of study for the past year—had brought in the white girl after she and her friends had robbed a pineapple vendor. Her wrists were bound with a zip tie, and she was hissing like a feral cat. When she tried to bite the officer, he jerked away. According to Bram, who mimicked the bass voice often used by African figures of authority in films, the officer said, "She is a demon, and you are looking for demons, and she is a white demon, so there was nowhere to take her but here."

"I paid him well," Bram told me, "because I have foresight."

"You hoped to work with him again?" I said.

"Indeed. She looked like a child who might escape, though she has done so more easily than I expected. I figured I'd encourage him to see a market in returning her. I've already called him, and he is on the lookout."

Bram then motioned me across the relatively long, rectangular room containing a table and his laptop, to a door. It opened on a small, windowless chamber with a cot, some blankets, a bottle of water, and a bucket.

"She escaped from here," he said. "There's no way out. But she told me that Mami Wata—a water siren often depicted as a snake charmer—would help her transform into a serpent and get free. It's hard not to wonder . . ."

He turned, eyeing me with clear wariness and jealousy—of his story and of Sola, I suspected—but perhaps also considering me as a potential ally against her, who was watching us, arms crossed and chin lowered.

I was trying to think of how to insert myself into this situation inextricably, and I said, "I know a pastor who might be able to help. He's knowledgeable and connected, though I'm sure you can reach out to pastors yourself."

"Actually," Bram replied, "I can't. I've bothered them so much for my research on street children that they're, well, they're rather sick of me. They won't even take my money, and that's saying something here."

"I can call him now," I offered, and he simultaneously shrugged and nodded.

On my way over, in the taxi, I'd stopped to buy a SIM card from a street vendor and had inserted it into my phone. I now dialed Oméga's number, and he answered on the second ring. He recalled the story of the girl and said that he'd be honored to help and knew where to take me. He just "happened to be free"—a serendipity that made me suspicious of what I might have that he could want. I gave him directions, and he said he would pick me up in an hour or so.

I conveyed all of this to Bram, who nodded without thanking me. He placed his knuckles to his lips in contemplation and paced a few steps like that.

"If I agree to share my notes with you," he said, "and if I agree to let you write about this, then we will have to come to an agreement."

"What sort of agreement?" I asked, holding back a smile.

"We'll have to sign a contract saying that I retain full intellectual rights and above all, film rights."

I understood his concern. He was certain that he'd struck gold and was more likely to turn a profit if I wrote about him, but he didn't want to lose control of the material.

"Wouldn't the film rights belong to the girl?" I asked.

"She's a minor," he said.

"Or to her family then?"

"I am, or will be, technically, her guardian."

Sola groaned behind us and walked out of the room, into the hallway.

Years ago, I'd read—in one of my mother's many books on how to live more peacefully—that when someone annoyed me, I should picture the more mature and thoughtful individual they would grow into and speak to that person instead, but with Bram all I could conjure up was a goaty, desiccated, neurotic professor: calculating, ranking his life's experiences, dividing them between wins and injustices.

I considered his proposal. He wasn't the first interviewee to express concern that he might lose film rights, and I knew that without signing a contract, my access to this story would be limited to what Sola might share with me at some later time.

"Sure," I said, and he snatched a notepad and began writing up the terms.

"Just something rudimentary," he told me, "but enough to affirm that our handshake has a legal basis."

We signed the basic condition that he would retain film rights to his story and the girl's, though I was fairly sure no court would view him as the proprietor of her experiences. He gleefully hurried to the table and began sorting papers.

"Where do you think your article will be published?"

"It's hard to say at this point. I'll have to work up a pitch."

"I've been translating and editing this all night. I'm basically trying to reduce hours of interviews with her down to a single coherent story."

"She answered questions for hours?"

"It took a lot of candy . . ."

He handed me a sheaf of papers and led me to a room he'd decorated as a lounge, with cushioned chairs and a cracked terrarium empty but for some kind of palm growing in a lump of soil. He then left to find Sola, and their voices reached me, staccato at first before easing to the solemn tones of shared concern.

On the first page, a photo was printed on computer paper in black and white. It struck me as insensitive: the girl's washed face, her pale eyes and stringy hair—the sort of image you'd expect of a child who'd been thrown into freezing water and was clambering out, looking up. The concrete room behind her blurred away, and her face seemed blank, waiting to be inhabited by the words I was about to read.

I crossed the ocean on the blade of a knife.

That where my story begin, so stop asking. Never was a mother. Never was no father but the Father, and He won't forgive me. Only the Demon want me. He hunt me in the street. Each time the preacher try to save me, God keep quiet, and I go back to the demon's arms. There is human flesh in my belly. Preachers take it out, but an empty belly mustn't stay empty, so the demon, he put it back in.

You not the first demon who catch me. Even if you trap my story in that little box, I will escape.

[. . .]

I was with Keicha and Marvine, on the edge of the market, in a comfortable piece of shadow when the fruit truck come. My stomach was in my eyes, and all it hold was those fat pineapples jiggling beneath the tarp. That's why he see me before I see him—the demon. I turn to make sure no police was spying us eating free dinner inside our heads, and there he was, whiter than a dead man in the rain, staring with eyes the color of a dead eye, the color of the grease on a puddle you never drink from.

I see Awax and Eudes, little boys, not yet proud of their cocks, good runners but not like Marvine—she yanké.[1] *She*

1. Strong, derived from the word Yankee. Despite the negative influence Americans exert on the Congo, Yankee has become a term for power. (All notes in this chapter are from the text of Bram Rees.)

have lupemba[2] *and speed so fast because she run in two worlds. You see just her scrap of skirt sailing and that pink bow in her hair. All of us go for different pineapple. The driver, he have wrench. He bang Eudes on the skull. Eudes always* mbakasa.[3] *He the sweetest, like little brother, even if he* yuma.[4] *He fall so fast I know he gone. The rest of us we get away, but I see the demon in the sunlight, watching.*

We find place to eat. We eating and crying. We eat till there blisters in our mouths and each golden bite hurts. I have half a pineapple and I see some older girls and run to sell it. That when I get jumped. Comes fast like being knocked down by wind. A man on me. Police man from the look of the sleeve I bite. He push my face in dirt, tie my hands, pull me up on my knees. Just in front, there's a dog drinking from a puddle, looking at me with Eudes's eyes. 'Don't drink that!' I shout as the man carry me past. Eudes have a weak stomach, always thirsty. Maybe that why he jump in this dog. To dog, even piss is whiskey. Except dogs don't last as long as street kids.

I flipped the pages back to the girl's photo. It now seemed to evoke the story I was reading—eyes so accepting

2. Good luck, also whiteness. This juxtaposition is striking: whiteness as strength and whiteness as evil. In post-independence Congo, whiteness is seen as the source of harm—the force that has kept many Congolese in servitude, with Western powers manipulating the government so as to exploit the Congo's resources. And yet whiteness also embodies savvy and power.

3. Weak and unable to find money.

4. Idiot.

of the faint light that they could be haunted or emptied to make space for determination.

I crossed the ocean on the blade of a knife.

Demon tell me this first time he catch and turn me white. It was police again. They came in when we were sleeping. Police hand on my ankle like snakebite.

Then I'm in a room with the demon. White skin, white hair, white eyes. Nothing in him have color. He was white. White like a hot sky.

He was speaking words I don't know. Then he talk le français, *but like with half a tongue, half a tongue with a bonbon on it. He switch to Lingala. Quarter tongue now.*

Where are you from? he ask first thing, the way you do, like only that matter.

Here.

But before? Where were you born?

In the sky, I tell him.

In the sky?

He don't believe me.

I come from the sky. I live in Kinshasa, but sometimes at night I fly to the forests and I dance with the spirits.

So you live in Kinshasa? he ask, not dumb—demons aren't dumb—but trying to trick me, to get me to say something he can use to enter me. But I come from the sky. That the kind of witch I am. Sky witch. Marvine took me to the old lady who told me that. She say that Mami Wata love sky witch because the wind makes the water move. Now we know. It give us power.

I bought you from the police, he tell me.

You not the first, I say.

It was expensive, he tell me.

Go cry blood, I say.

The demon, he undress me. He drag me in a room so small—small as my heart when he inside it—and he pull off my clothes. He throw me in water hot as rain from hell. He was cooking me. Staring. Big white hungry eyes. Like mean cat watching fat man at dinner.

But then, like he want to chat up his soup, he say, You're white. He point. Where are you from?

I look down and scream. My color wash off. I scream and hold my skin. I scream for help. I scream for spirits. I even give scream for the Father, but He don't answer, busy with the holy people. He already know I am witch.

The door creaked as Sola slipped in like a double agent. I jumped a little, so caught up that I felt guilty. I had goose bumps, and many thoughts—above all concerning who the man was. I couldn't stop thinking of Richmond Hew, of what both Terra and the disaffected conservationist had said about his appetite for girls, and I wondered if he sometimes left the rainforest and spent time in Kinshasa.

"How's the reading coming?" she asked.

"It's disturbing."

She sat down in the chair next to me and studied my face.

"The look in your eye," she said, "please make it that of a man searching not for the next great story but rather for an abandoned child."

"I know," I said too quickly.

She put her hand on my forearm.

"This is a little girl, and she's out there, being hunted

down by police right now. She's been sexually abused. She's been a child prostitute. And when the police catch her, they might rape her before they bring her here."

"I understand," I said, though I hadn't really. When I'd arrived, I'd wondered if Sola had a genuine interest in me or whether she'd invited me as a barrier against Bram. I realized that maybe none of this was about me.

"Bram is so fascinated with the demon," she said, "that he doesn't seem the least bit bothered that the girl saw her friend get murdered for trying to feed himself."

I nodded gravely, embarrassed that this death hadn't registered with me more—no doubt the fault of the text's faux literary style. After a pause, Sola told me that she'd just listened to some of the recording in Lingala.

"The girl actually said 'I came here on a knife.' And then she changed it later, when Bram asked her about the ocean, to 'I crossed the ocean on a knife.' He asked, 'What kind of knife,' and she said, 'I crossed the ocean on the blade of a knife and I used it to cut open this little girl's heart.'"

I ran my thumb along the edges of the papers.

"I was wondering about that. The translation's dialect is hard to place."

She laughed soundlessly, almost sadly.

"Years back, Bram spent some time in Jamaica, as a research assistant for a professor, and he fancies himself an expert on its culture and literature. He thought that translating the girl's Lingala and street French into standard English would be a misrepresentation, and he decided that this"—she gestured derisively toward the papers—"this lewd approximation of Jamaican dialect would render her character."

Though hushed, her voice conveyed so much emotion

that I found myself wondering if she had some Jamaican heritage herself.

"Anyway." She squeezed my arm. "Thank you for helping with this and for calling the pastor. I'll let you get back to reading."

As she stood to leave, my desire lurched within me, a bodily motion, though I held still. I hated attraction like this and often, in response, I worked my mind into a disciplined state and deconstructed my perceptions, convincing myself that I knew nothing about the person, that—in terms of raw data—she hardly existed behind my projections. But doing this also made me look more closely, and I wanted to look now, to ask questions, but the door was already closing.

I settled my gaze on the page: this slight connection to a child whose humanity seemed no more than the idea of a child and yet could connect me—if I made myself sensitive to it—to Sola, who herself was less a person in my mind than the idea of potential I loved so much.

There was the line again. It glowed like the light emitted from a bulb whose incandescing prevents you from seeing the object at its source.

I crossed the ocean on the blade of a knife.

But I will never tell you the secrets of the streets. Magic is no choice. We do it to survive. Hunger get so bad your feet turn to roots so you can live on the juice of the earth. You walk past little trees and they are children. Skinny branches for arms. Heads a bush of leaves gobbling up sunlight. We do that for an hour or two, hoping no greedy cook come and cut us down to make fire in her kitchen.

You think I don't know things. I live with my écurie.[5] *We have secret places. We have friends. The* mokonzi[6] *love us and bring presents from far away. At night, we fly to jungle and dance with spirits. Or we fly to Europe. We drink blood from diamond cups, eat sweet pudding from human flesh, pudding so thick and strong it run into our bones and make them creak like the hot metal of old truck, when you hiding under it.*

I tell you this story for your bonbons, but I will kill you, white demon. Mami Wata and I will cut your throat and pour your blood into a diamond glass, and we will drink it and laugh. She will turn me into a snake and I will leave through these walls.

I closed my eyes, commanding my brain to remember what Sola had asked of me—that I was reading about a twelve-year-old child abandoned here. It was hard to see her as blameless when she sounded so certain, so determined to kill.

Again I thought of the white man who'd bathed her—who'd maybe been trying to save her—and of Hew, and then of Oméga's words about how the spirits left nothing to chance. But I was inclined to believe that the story we wanted to tell led us, shifting the focus of the world.

I crossed the ocean on the blade of a knife.

The streets call me. My sisters dance and the spirits hear them. They bring me. They cut the sky in two and let me in.

5. Gang; literally "stable" in French, as in "horse stable."

6. Big men; powerful men.

I know you want to hear about the graveyard of souls, because you want to know how I will kill you. You should be giving me libulu ya mbongo.[7] *No? Some* pelouse[8] *maybe? No? Then give me the whole bag of bonbons.*

Okay, it's easy. You do the business as usual. You spread the legs for mbongo, *but you be sure to use the* kapote.[9] *He do his thing fast. It always fast, not like the older boys in the street, the ones who like you, who have nothing to run home to. The* mokonzi, *they just want something extra. So we girls catch their poison in the* kapote, *and we knot it, and we take it to the graveyard.*

We get down between the headstones and make sure no demon is close. We dig holes and then we stick crooked branches in the ground and hang the kapote.

At first, nothing happen. Those ugly bags of man sap hang in the dark. Then the moon shine in them, and the light inside the rubber start, like spark in dry grass. It get bigger until it bright like to blind us and we see the demon seed squirming inside. Then, from every side of the graveyard, the spirits of the mokonzi *appear, walking like they have broken knees, arms out like this, like zombie, tripping and reaching . . .*

My cell rang, followed by honking outside. Oméga had arrived. I didn't want to stop reading, but making him wait wouldn't be respectful.

I stood and called to Bram and Sola that I was leaving.

---

7. A whole lot of money (*mbongo*).

8. Marijuana, literally "lawn" in French.

9. Condom.

"It's no problem," he said, appearing in the doorway, "you can finish later."

"Do you mind if I take this copy?" I held up the manuscript.

"I do. I'd like to retain control of the material until I have a polished draft and we've finalized our contractual agreement."

I hadn't expected this and glanced at the pages, unsure of what to say.

He came nearer and slid them from my hand. He smiled, standing uncomfortably close and showing two rows of small, straight, very white teeth.

"Be patient," he said. "A cliffhanger is nothing more than an interruption."

6

THE CHURCH OF THE ALBINO PROPHET

The traffic was dense, the thoroughfares particularly crowded with hulking trucks—Frankenstein vehicles resurrected over and over, assembled from an army of fallen Lazaruses, their pieces bolted, hammered, wired in place. The sky was, after all, white with the haze of unmitigated exhaust, and the big trucks, as they struggled to accelerate, left dark fog banks through which we drove.

My dream returned, the blinding mist, the gravity of the vast current palpable in the night. The Congo River ran flush with Kinshasa, replenished by hundreds of tributaries—a watery labyrinth spanning the equator and draining an eighth of the African continent. And here, right before the river pummeled down to the sea, it separated two national capitals that had once been part of the Kongo Empire: the Republic of Congo's Brazzaville, a city of two million, and the Democratic Republic of Congo's Kinshasa—eleven million strong: labyrinths within labyrinths. But this river wasn't the phantom waterway from my dream the night before. That was another, almost as big, maybe even mistier, from my childhood.

Oméga was explaining that if a white street girl had been possessed by a white demon, she would eventually find her way to a famed *prophète* who knew how to do battle with such demons, since he'd been born under the spell of one.

"His story is unlike that of any other pastor. He's *un albinos.* Such people are common in Africa—more so than elsewhere—and yet there's no more unfortunate thing here. Some witch doctors say that their flesh is magic and eating it will heal you or give you good fortune. Others say that the albino is a source of evil and albinism is contagious. Albino children are sometimes sold. Even adults can be captured and their body parts used for ceremonies."

He sighed, with the faint, resigned smile of one considering life's absurd cruelty.

"I've never really understood, but so many people die of starvation that I suppose it doesn't take much of an excuse to eat something—whether a Pygmy or an albino. Maybe many Africans know that our sun will burn albinos—that they're not made to survive here—so we simply can't bear the thought of wasting fresh meat."

He laughed, as if he'd been leading up to this joke all along, and slapped his knee, but as soon as I joined in, he stopped.

"That's how your people see us, isn't it?" he asked.

"How?" I said, a laugh still on my lips, turned, no doubt, into a grimace.

He studied me a moment longer before chuckling, as if his question were the joke. He turned his palm up, lifting it slightly, the motion evocative of a shrug.

"Regardless," he said, "this *prophète*—you can't imagine his faith. His family throws him out during the war. He lives in the street but is not eaten. He is cross-eyed yet learns to read. He studies the Bible. He finds a home in churches and he preaches. He does battle with the demons afflicting him and overcomes the evil of his birth. Rising victorious, he prays to cure others, and his followers enjoy health and abundance."

"He's a friend of yours?" I asked, feeling guarded and somewhat shaken.

"Ah, no. We're competitors."

Our Land Rover swerved off the road, down a dusty side street, and another, between low, crumbling walls and deep gutters, and again, into a small lot before the immense concrete carcass of a church—an unfinished hull: unadorned, rain streaked, like the broken temple of a martial god eroding into dust.

The sermon was already underway. The hall was long, with coarse concrete pillars and flimsy, multicolored plastic chairs, and at the end, on a wooden platform overhung with blue tarpaulins, the colorless pastor invoked the space above him, in which motes blinked through shafts of light between the rusting metal sheets of the partial roof. The congregation cried out and flayed the air with their arms, as if demons swarmed about their heads like moths.

We found a space amid the standing bodies that were less crowded than they'd appeared from a distance, easily outnumbered by the plastic chairs. The albino pastor was preaching, and Oméga stood close and whispered.

"Keep an eye out. The girl might be here or might come in."

I glanced around. Crouched against a wall in a dark

corner was a dusty child. Another rested on the floor beneath an exposed staircase. Neither were white.

"Street children often sleep in churches," he told me. "This creates a symbiotic relationship. The pastor can cast out their demons and prove that he has *l'onction*—unction, power, grease—"

"So he's greased with the spirit," I said.

"Exactly!" Oméga's eyes widened with pleasure.

"And do you have *l'onction*?"

"Do I ever! But even I haven't exorcised a white demon. That would bring quite the audience. He would gain followers. So we must be subtle. We do not mention the girl until we have an audience. He may be afraid that we'll take her away. Oh, and don't tell anyone that I'm a pastor."

"Okay. Don't tell them I'm a journalist."

"I'll say that I'm your translator."

The chalky walls and pillars were decorated only with the whorls of the warped plywood forms into which the concrete had been poured, except for a few places where photocopied images showed the *prophète* healing white people.

"Should we say that I've come from America to be healed?"

"Don't mock. I have similar photos in my church. I got some recently on my last trip to Chicago. Healing *mundele* shows power."

"Sorry," I said. "But isn't that kind of racist?"

"No, it's the opposite of racism, since the healer must walk through the hordes of oppressive and hateful whites to lay his hands on them and bring them peace. How can you deny the love and power in that?"

"I can't," I said, feeling utterly stupid.

"And you really have no fear of God?" he asked, exasperated.

"No. I don't." I shrugged apologetically.

"So would—I fear even saying this—would you spit on the face of Jesus?"

"No."

"Why?"

"Out of respect for believers."

"And if no one would ever know?"

"I still wouldn't. Because I would have no reason to."

"If someone put a gun to your head and shouted, 'Spit!'"

"Yes. I would."

"Would you be afraid?"

I thought about it as I tried to make out what the albino pastor was doing beyond the thicket of waving arms.

"I'd be uncomfortable, maybe," I said.

"And why?"

"Because I've been trained to fear deep inside of me."

"So you've been trained to have some seed of faith?"

"I've been brainwashed like most humans."

"How do you know that it's training, that it's not a seed of true faith, as is written in Ecclesiastes—a gift from God?"

"I can't prove it one way or the other, but I believe society trains us."

"You believe," he said, his whisper rising a little with irritation, "but you do not know. So you would not go spitting and pissing all over God's great works—on church steps, on statues of Jesus, on crosses and on holy men?"

"That probably wouldn't be the best use of my time."

"Yes. You simply do not want to admit that there is a grain of faith in you. That you fear deep within yourself that there are other forces in the world. Be careful, because those who do not believe end up in suffering they cannot explain."

"I believe we all suffer in ways we can't explain."

Our whispered debate had drawn scowls from members of the congregation, and I asked Oméga, "Isn't it rude to speak during the sermon?"

He made a dismissive gesture and said, "The style here is so histrionic. It annoys me. And the way they pray—flapping about like injured birds—they look as if they're trying to wave God down as he drives past on the highway."

The preacher had left the platform, and people were praying in hushed voices now, standing or sitting, or touching each other, clutching hands and rocking. The mass seemed to be ending in a sort of quiet time.

"You should tell the prophet that you are the girl's uncle," Oméga said. "That will keep things simple. You have come to bring her home to America and you would like to pay him to cast out her demons before you go. He can't refuse that. And if you really want to play the part, have him lay hands on you too. I doubt you'll regret it."

Congregants were lining up to meet with their *prophète*—a term that I was beginning to think wasn't so rare. He'd withdrawn behind a crimson tapestry guarded by a thin young woman in a silvery sparkling dress and matching head wrap. Each time she pulled back the heavy cloth to let in the faithful, I glimpsed a hallway of exposed concrete.

As Oméga went to speak with her, I kept my distance, pacing toward the wide doorway that framed the twilight. When I glanced back, the *prophète*'s assistant had turned from Oméga to evaluate me. Though she had the slight features of a girl, her posture was almost soldierly, her jaw jutting with authority and disapproval.

I again faced the doorway, and now a figure appeared in it, an old man, bony and stooped, draped with hanging cloth that, in the dark, resembled robes. He began to say what sounded like *Monsieur* and I was almost certain that the following word was *Richmond*—that he'd questioningly murmured "Monsieur Richmond?" He neared, staring hard. His eyes were ashen with cataracts.

Suddenly, he hobbled past, his disjointed gait across the hall marked by the clacking of his short cane. As he reached the purple curtain, the young woman pulled it back, and he disappeared.

Having finished speaking with Oméga, she motioned him to a row of white plastic chairs against the far wall. I joined, realizing that in my surprise I hadn't actually paid close attention to what the old man was wearing—robes or a sheet bunched up like a toga, or rags. Kinshasa was exacting, and I felt the swift onset of fatigue, the strain on my nerves from the perpetual stench of exhaust, of dust ground through with contaminants.

I said nothing, sitting next to Oméga as one by one the congregants were let past the tapestry, or departed from behind it. Every now and then children came in alone or in small groups, barefoot or in broken shoes, occasionally holding a grubby plastic bag with something inside.

"Since we have this time," Oméga said, "I will tell you about Richmond Hew."

I tried not to show my surprise, but the conjunction of his statement and the interaction at the door gave me the impression of unspooling delirium. My mother once told me that when I was feverish or tired as a child, I sometimes hallucinated. On days like these, in places like this, I felt that perceptual fragility. Sometimes, exhausted, in the instant before drifting off, I heard far-off voices, discerning their rhythms and notes of inflection, but rarely their words.

Thankfully, Oméga occupied our brief silence, catching his breath after a tired sigh, and then kept on.

"If you're interested in Hew, you must already know he is not a good man. He's been in the country thirty years at least, and his patronage system is large. The organizations would cut him off if he didn't give them what they want. If they need a park, he knows who to pay, and in no time they can announce that they've saved part of the rainforest. Does any of this sound familiar?"

"It does. But is there truth in . . ." I silenced myself mid-gesticulation, not wanting to put words in his mouth.

"I know," he told me. "The stories are bad, especially those about the girls—fourteen, thirteen, sometimes younger. I've heard he's afraid of HIV, so when he arrives in a new village, he picks a virgin and pays the family to make sure she's available only for him. As proof, I can give you a letter that tribal chiefs sent to the ministry of the environment. At least a dozen have signed it. But it's just a worn-out, handwritten piece of paper and nothing makes it official."

He shot a glance at the line of congregants and the young woman in silver, and grunted with impatience.

The old man in robes—or just rags—hadn't reappeared, and I was now sure I'd imagined his words. I'd wanted so badly to blaze an incriminating trail that, in a lapse of delusional weariness, I'd overlaid his utterance in Lingala with Hew's name.

I steadied my mind with a long exhalation, measured my next breath, and then asked, "Do you know if Terra's disappearance has anything to do with Hew?"

"Of course it does. He has played that situation well. She was working with villagers to protect gorillas, and Parks International approached her about making a park. When she refused, Hew was called in."

"Do you think she's still alive?"

"It's not likely, but it's possible she's being kept prisoner until after everyone she worked with has been paid off and the park has been made."

"And you knew her well?"

"Terra? Yes. Very." He lowered his voice and leaned in close. "She was my lover for a while. When she first went out there, she was young—twenty-three or four. Very brave. Every now and then, when she came back from America, she would bring a different boyfriend. The men would play the adventurer—that much was clear—dressed like they were going to discover the source of the Congo River! They drank with the locals and slept with young women in the villages, and then she kicked them out for undermining her power. I think she was too focused on her work to care about the infidelities. By the time I met her, when I was doing conflict resolution in the east—that's what I have my degree in, by the way—she was lonely. I recall"—he laughed with pleasure—"that she wanted me to use a condom. I never had, and I told her that doing so seemed sad and unnatural, and that besides, it was against my faith.

"'What faith?' she asked. That was before I became a pastor, and she was like that—never a hesitation to say what she thought.

"'I am Catholic,' I told her, because I was back then, before I realized it limited me to being a spectator to foreign traditions, and she said"—he stifled a laugh here—"'you have children with three women that I know of.' So I responded, 'Who am I to turn my back on the ways of my ancestors. Never mind. Give me the condom. I will make an exception. With a white woman, God plays by different rules.'"

He slapped his thigh and his laughter broke free. Across the hall, the young assistant glowered, and the remaining congregants shook their heads.

"Ah," Oméga told me, "she was my first white woman. Only then did I know I had truly survived the war."

A child came to the church entrance, shirtless, in pants torn off at the knees. The afternoon was at an end, the sun already on its vertical dive, hurtling toward an equatorial sunset as the shadows in the street lengthened visibly.

Oméga cleared his throat and said, "A white woman in America is one thing, but a white woman in the Congo is another experience altogether. I recall seeing you in the airport with Sola and having had that thought. How I envied you."

It seemed reasonable that he saw Sola as white, since we likely take note of what is different from ourselves. I could discern that she had nonwhite ancestry, so diluted that it might be Latin or Middle Eastern, though—perhaps because we'd been traveling to the Congo—I'd been persuaded that her family origins were, at least in part, African. Oméga had no doubt identified her Caucasian extraction, which, admittedly, appeared preponderant.

"I believe Terra would make a good story as well," he now said. "But if you write about her as Hew's victim, remember that she had her vision for the lands where she held power, and not all the people agreed with her."

He hesitated, carefully choosing his words, and I wondered how—if he did become minister of the environment—my investigation might play into his hands.

"Those who opposed her," he continued, "suffered and a few had to move away. This is the thing with white people here. They make the news that Americans hear about them. Terra only ever told the world about those who loved her."

I considered this, that she might herself be a Kurtz, with her abilities to move through cultures or to manifest them within herself—to seduce the general or me, or the people among whom she lived, or simply overpower them.

Until now, the article I'd been envisioning revolved around Hew in his jungle lair, but it would be more compelling if it were about two Kurtzes at odds, one a publicity virtuoso and the other a secretive wielder of ruthless power.

The church was growing dark, and somewhere, in the unfinished roof, a bird cawed hesitantly.

"After our flight," Oméga said, "the way you talked about literature, it stayed with me. I intend to write my story, but I'm looking for the tools to make sure it's a best seller. What do you think those are?"

"I've published a few books," I told him, "but they weren't best sellers. I like stories in which characters try to wake up. A lot of novels and movies and TV series are about normal people reacting to extraordinary, usually extraordinarily bad, situations. Aliens invade, and a bunch of average humans fight back and reiterate American triumphalism. It's all about overcoming something evil and contrary to our way of life, which we pretend is freedom and justice. The introspection is predictable—basically just cheerleading for one's own survival and dominance."

My cell phone chimed with a message. It was Sola, asking me if I wanted to have dinner, and I texted back quickly, *Yes! At my hotel? Or other suggestions?*

Oméga waited, head bowed in consideration.

"What interests me," I continued, "is when a character's internal world demands a transformation of the outside world. I'm drawn to characters who have shaped an internal conviction and . . ."

"Do you have this conviction?"

"Some days, I think so. Maybe that's why I want to see it written. At times, I feel a spark of belief, of something I could give my life to . . ."

Above our heads, two crossing electrical wires began to quiver. A small rat was in a tightrope routine—advancing, pausing, extending its head a bit and sniffing, before proceeding and once again hesitating where the black cords crossed. Then suddenly it forged on to another dark corner.

My cell phone bleeped. *At the hotel, in two hours?*

I messaged back, *Yes! Looking forward to it.*

"There is this thing you do not know about me," Oméga said. "Since you have been so open with me, I will tell you a secret."

His voice sounded truly sad for the first time since I'd known him.

"My father," he told me, "he was white."

"*Un homme blanc*? Like me?"

He gave a dispirited shrug.

"White enough. His father was white. I, too, am white."

I looked at him closely. I narrowed my eyes. In the dusk, his skin didn't seem quite so dark, as if he spent less time in the sun than other people here, but I wasn't sure if I was imagining this. Maybe he was trying to connect with me, to establish a bond between us as two *hommes blancs*.

Another grungy boy had run in from the street to the young woman in silver, placing something in her palm before flitting back outside. Perhaps thinking herself unobserved, she slouched a little and put her hand just below her diaphragm, wincing faintly, as if in pain or hunger.

Oméga called to her.

"*Mama*," he said, "am I not white?"

She immediately regained her composure. In the ebbing light, her face was a bright mask of evaluation.

"Yes, I see it now," she said. "You are a white. Do you not know that the prophet is tired of being bothered by *mundele*?"

As she turned away, Oméga laughed nervously. I sensed that he regretted his disclosure but couldn't backpedal.

"My friend," he said in a suddenly tired voice, "we are always more than one thing and must see ourselves as such. Faithful sinners, or men of reason who act in folly. We face not just spiritual threats—the slough of despond, the hill of difficulties, the vanity fair—but the scars of colonialism. By education, I understand many of the white ways of being, but never fully from the inside, and yet I am no longer entirely inside my own people's ways of thinking. Maybe none of us are. It's hard to say who truly is, who doesn't act without another part of himself judging the nature of that action. Even the pleasure I've had with white women—I've questioned that. You whites admire beauties from other countries. Why can Africans not do so? Why is connecting with a white woman always about our need for power and not simply the pleasure of newness, of understanding a person from far away? But there is obvious power in all of these situations, for the white as for the African."

The young woman in silver had disappeared behind the tapestry. A congregant in a sagging suit slipped from behind it and shuffled outside.

"Tomorrow," Oméga said, glancing at his watch, "there's

a person we should meet. To have survived so long in the rainforest, Hew has learned to get things cheaply from smugglers, especially during the war. In the Congo, people fear what is unnatural—the albino but also the dwarf and the cripple. Evil touched them, yet they survived. Even police and inspectors avoid them. That is why dwarves and cripples do much of the smuggling across the river between Kinshasa and Brazzaville. I will take you to meet a man. He will help us with both Hew and your little witch."

No more congregants had come out. Nor had the old man in robes.

One of the city's lone, survivalist crickets trilled, the naked concrete amplifying its lonely entreaties for a mate.

"We must concede defeat," Oméga said in a tired voice. "Maybe I was recognized. Maybe I should have let you wait alone. I believe that the pastor has prayed and God has revealed our reasons to him."

We stood, and I followed him slowly to the door, still hoping that the young woman in silver would reappear from behind the crimson tapestry.

"Thank you for sharing your thoughts on the best seller," Oméga murmured and touched the collar of his shirt, just below his throat, where his scar was. "I will meditate on your insights, but my novel will have less to do with my convictions or the power of my will than the proof of God's love. Every step on the road to this moment—even small, mysterious disappointments like this one—each one has been a miracle. Even this scar. Especially this scar. It is a blessing. I touch it to thank God and I remember. The cutting of the skin can be the sparing of the heart."

7

A NIGHT WITH SOLA

At the hotel, with forty minutes to spare, I sat in my room with my laptop. There was no news about Terra, and I again researched Richmond Hew, hoping to find something substantial this time. Online, his name seemed like an elemental gas, atmospheric in its prevalence yet difficult to pinpoint in concentration. Despite his more than three decades making parks, the only photo of him that came up was a shadowy image of a man turning away from the camera, lifting his arm as if gesturing to the rainforest canopy, his shoulder blocking half his face. He had a pronounced brow and hair so pale it could have been white or a very light blond. The same photo appeared on a number of conservation websites, and on one of them it was attached to an article about a different conservationist whose name I didn't recognize and whose projects were in Congo–Brazzaville. I wondered how Hew, who worked with so many big NGOs, could be so elusive online, as if he'd feared that his misdeeds might come to light and he'd known that, without his image, people would have nowhere to aim their outrage, and it would dissolve against the unknown.

It was time. I arrived in the lobby just as Sola was coming in, wearing the jeans and black long-sleeved shirt she'd had on earlier. She kissed my cheeks in the French fashion, and I asked how she was doing.

"The police haven't found the girl," she told me.

"I had no luck either," I said, wondering if she ever spoke about herself.

We walked into the hotel restaurant that was quiet but for the murmured conversations of a dozen or so diners and the clink of their forks. The polished wooden maître d' stand was unmanned, and she passed it, choosing a corner table.

"It turns out that Bram's mother is sick and he's going to the Netherlands tomorrow. I don't know for how long, but I want to find the girl before he returns."

"What does he expect?" I asked. "He can't study her indefinitely."

"The problem is that he actually sort of believes the demon story."

"You're kidding me."

"He will pretend that he doesn't in front of you, but he's one of those anthropologists who accepts that the truth lies in worldviews. His father was a missionary and a doctor, and Bram grew up in the eastern Congo, near Lubutu. His father partook of local rituals so that he could, quote, 'find a place for Christ beneath the dense canopy of animism.'"

"So, to some degree, Bram believes he's actually studying a demon?"

"I'm not sure. He contradicts himself often and then

justifies doing so by saying that he struggles with the hybridized worldviews he grew up in."

"I see," I said, and did understand—believed, in fact, that all worldviews were hybridized, that our brains were archaeological layers if not geologic strata, not only of belief but of instinct, so that at the surface we played at being rational, modern creatures while our viscera churned with primeval fears.

I talked about this a bit, saying something along the lines of "Dignity arises—for me at least—from the grace with which we handle our contradictions . . ." but my words drifted off when I realized I was plagiarizing an article from my news feed on how to embrace career failure. I also realized that I was about to dis Bram. And in truth, maybe what I was calling grace was merely artful dissimulation. Besides, I didn't trust my distrust of him, since I had too much incentive not to like him.

"It would be one thing," Sola told me, "if Bram spoke with the girl compassionately while trying to help her, but he is infusing the story with his own expectations, mythologizing it, and that makes it easier for him to isolate her."

We fell silent as the waiter neared. The menu was high cuisine in the French tradition, the prices stressful even by the standards of Kinshasa, where a premium was put on every piece of meat to prevent the meager supply from vanishing into the hands of the famished populace. The waiter took our orders and sauntered off.

"Where did you grow up?" I asked, and she appeared to flinch, though maybe I imagined it—or maybe she shared my belief that regional categories ultimately revealed little about us as individuals.

"I was born in Saint Louis," she said, "but my father was a businessman and we moved often. Then my parents split, and I lived with my mother in the DC area."

She went on to explain that she had a master's in social work and another in public policy, and had studied both anthropology and global affairs as an undergraduate at Yale.

"You began working overseas as a result of your studies?" I asked, unsure of why she sounded so reticent.

"I guess so. I spent time in the Middle East, India and east Africa, and when the Congo War started, I came here. I spoke decent Swahili, which made it easy to work in the eastern Congo, and I picked up some Lingala. There was no lack of jobs coordinating development work, and I increasingly specialized in information gathering. I felt useful, and I liked feeling useful, and after the financial crash, it wasn't as if there were a lot of jobs back home."

"That's the main reason you stayed overseas?"

Our bisques arrived, and we ate slowly, the way Westerners do in the Congo—to check the freshness, the cleanliness, the thoroughness of the cooking, or to see exactly what was in there.

"I guess I went through a period of disillusionment with the US. My older brother had a hard time and got in a lot of trouble. His problems more or less led to my parents' separation. They put pressure on me to be perfect, as if to prove that what happened with him wasn't their fault, that they weren't bad people or bad parents, which they weren't. So I guess I wanted distance from their expectations but also from the US. I was angry about how my brother had fallen apart. I'd seen what punishment can do to people."

She took a deep breath and her exhalation was

accompanied by a tremor, as if deep within her body she were giving herself a shake, letting all this go.

She stirred her soup and took a spoonful.

"So how is the pursuit of Kurtz coming along?" she asked.

"Slowly."

"But it must help to have a villain," she said, a hint of teasing in her voice. "Is that what drives you?"

I pushed back my empty bowl slowly, almost genteelly—I felt, observing myself—though I was buying time to collect my thoughts.

"I've always liked that wording," I told her, "that something drives us, even though we generally speak of our drives as if we create them. But I believe that we are the product of our drives, and that makes them hard to talk about, since they precede us . . ."

"I get it," she said, "but you're talking about the idea of something that drives you, not what actually drives you."

"That's it. I struggle with that question. Don't we all?"

"I suppose so. But most people don't live such extreme lives."

She watched me, not with intensity or judgment, but with a sort of detached interest mingled with fatigue. On the airplane, I'd spoken with greater ease, thinking she was flitting through my life.

"I suspect," she said, "that people often ask what you're running away from."

"Is that what you want to ask?"

"Only if it's relevant. It's an example."

"I grew up poor," I told her. "My father was a thug. I won't go into it, but he was often involved in crime. I wrote a book about it." I gestured vaguely, over my shoulder, as if to say it was behind me. "He'd try to go clean, start a business and get his life in order, but he'd manage his money poorly or live beyond his means, and then he'd be broke again and fall back into crime."

The waiter arrived, placing chicken risotto before Sola, steak and greens before me. We began to eat, and then I continued.

"Anyway, for me, as a kid, breaking the law wasn't a big deal. My father used to tell me that the only things that were illegal were the ones you got caught doing. So I thought a lot about how to get away with my crimes. I stole, rarely in excess and not to survive, just to feel important. I also loved books and did fairly well in school. I realized that the people around me saw this. I'll be frank. They saw a young white man with blond hair and blue eyes, and I think they saw themselves. They saw hope. And even when I stole from them and they asked me questions—never accusing, just testing the subject—I directed the talk to literature, history, philosophy."

"You were a very literary thief," she said, smiling, her expression gentle now.

"Yes. I was. And back then, on one hand, survival drove me. On the other, my loves and passions did, and I couldn't really explain those. I still can't. I loved literature and ideas the way I loved a perfect moment in nature. But I was also very aware of injustice. I was aware of how I could hide behind this . . . this face. I knew that I could disappear into the idea others had of me, and that didn't seem to be a way of existing. So resentment and some guilt also drove me, and then there were these moments, either in nature or in a room where there was the right quality of light and silence, a sort of deepening of presence, when I didn't need anything or have to be anything for someone else. I felt as if I emptied into the moment and, by becoming an absence, I experienced the world. I began to live for those moments. My life became—or has become, I guess—a sort of choreography to get myself close to that stillness—anywhere, in any landscape or city, even in the minutes between meetings. People often ask me why I can't stay still, and I wish they could feel this connection that may be the closest thing I know to love. I feel it with the earth and the sunlight, and also in moments when I am in motion, in those places where the tension of travel breaks and I am suspended between two points on the earth while feeling the invitation of both. I feel it when I'm not this face for others but just the world I'm in."

I closed my eyes, bothered—trying to test in my mind whether my words were true—and already caught with the desire to leave, to step away from whatever I might be becoming in her eyes. I wasn't sure what else to say—that I struggled with journalism, craving isolation. I often liked my meetings with people best afterward, when I could feel their impact within myself and see how I had changed.

She touched my hand where it rested on the table, and I became aware of how long my eyes had been closed.

"Thank you for sharing that," she said. "You don't have to say more."

"I'm sorry. I didn't realize I'd—"

"Please don't apologize."

"I must have been sitting like this long enough for you to escape."

She withdrew her hand, took her purse and stood.

"I'll be back in a moment. For real."

She waved to the waiter, and he pointed her toward the bathroom. Then I motioned to him, and he began preparing the bill, which I'd already calculated in my head, realizing how quickly I would exceed my budget here, since few editors could fathom the prices in a country with a destroyed infrastructure and no subsidies.

From the back of the room, a figure seemed to impinge dimly on my periphery, and then all at once a man was at my elbow, standing nearly behind me. He placed his fingertips on the table and leaned down, speaking close to my ear.

"If you are here for Vladimir," he said in an eastern European accent, "you should be more discreet."

"I'm not here for Vladimir."

"You are not here for Vladimir?"

From what little I could make out, the man speaking in my ear was one of those white men with the crooked, coldly shaven jaws I'd been accustomed to seeing during the war.

"I don't even know who Vladimir is," I told him.

"You were looking for a man who met with Vladimir."

"I was? I have no idea what you're talking about."

"Did you not ask at the bar yesterday after a certain man?"

"At the bar?" I said, as if trying to recall if I had—since this was interesting after all—though I hadn't.

"Do you want to find Vladimir?" he asked.

"I don't want to bother him," I said, afraid that I might say the wrong thing or that the stranger behind me was holding a weapon. "But if he can help me find the man—"

"Who is that man?"

"Richmond Hew."

"Ah. So then you are looking for Vladimir?"

"I guess so. Yes. I'm looking for Vladimir."

The hand he'd rested on the table withdrew and reached into his jacket. My pulse ratcheted up and though I feared his next action, I was now more alarmed that a valve might burst inside my chest. He took out a folded scrap of paper and placed it next to my dirty fork.

"Vladimir says next time go straight to him. Do not ask at the bar. He does not like intrigue."

The man turned and walked away, and though I wanted a clearer look at his face, I was afraid to glance back. Sola returned from the bathroom and sat down. The waiter brought the bill, and, to my relief, she insisted on splitting it.

"Here's the thing," she said, appearing uneasy now, and I was certain she would say something about Bram or her availability. Without putting her elbows on the table, she positioned her hands in a gesture of holding, her palms facing each other and her fingers spread.

"What you said makes sense to me. I have my convictions. I know what they are. But when I try to convey them, I need a personality—or a persona—or just to be someone others can understand. That personality is the problem. It's as if the human face with its words and personal stories is too weak of a connection to transmit the depth and urgency of feeling. When I hear you speak, this is what I think of—how the personality becomes more important than the forces shaping it, than even what drives me. I create the personality to connect with others, and that personality somehow fools me, almost parasitically, into believing in its primacy—not because of what I feel but because it's what others see. It is their connection to me. There is no way to bypass it to share what matters."

She lowered her eyes, her fingers still extended, caught in an exquisite hesitation, and how true her words were, that even as she was trying to crack open or dissolve the face I saw, or imbue it—make the forces that created her somehow immanent in her expressions and gestures—I was seeing her fingers, held slightly before her heart, conjuring or entreating.

"I lose equilibrium," she said, more softly, and lowered her hands, as if they'd failed her. "The personality makes me lose my equilibrium. Maybe that's because of how much is at stake when we try to tell anything about ourselves. We expose ourselves while coming into a power relationship with other ways of being. In the conflicts that arise, the forces that shape me don't get hurt. They feel less like matter than energy. But the personality does, the part of myself I identify as me, and suddenly that feels so much more important than everything else, and I try to affirm it against threats to it, so I guess . . . I guess what I'm saying is that I don't want the usual pains to lock me into an identity. I aspire to being in the room without trying to convince anyone of what I am."

I was listening, fascinated by her words but also distracted by my interaction with the man who'd just approached me. My adrenaline was crashing, my body exhausted and my fingers trembling. Now that she was finally engaged and speaking, I could see that she realized I wasn't fully present, and she looked down quickly.

"I'm sorry," I said.

"Why?"

"I'm interested in what you're saying. It's just that I had a strange interaction while you were in the bathroom. A man mistook me for someone else."

"Ah. A case of all white faces looking alike?"

"I guess. He was actually white, but I believe that one of the Congolese at the bar directed him to me, so maybe my generic white face is to blame."

"And you're fine now?" she asked, looking more at ease.

"Yes. In fact, what you're saying is true," I said, almost stammering with the effort to calm my mind. "I used to wonder why I was so impulsively rude in social settings—why I'd suddenly say things to shock others without planning to. Hearing you speak made me think of the years it took me to realize that I had a visceral hatred of roles. Even when I was trying to belong, I hated the performance. And this feeling has only gotten worse. I increasingly find it hard to read books. I see the performance in them—of authority, even of conviction, or goodness and innocence."

I stopped. Her eyes were so bright I couldn't look at them without feeling exposed. I hated that I'd interrupted her and gone on talking about myself—a nervous tic and my usual reaction to anxiety—but I understood now why we'd found it so easy to speak on the plane, despite the chattering in my brain, the mechanical need to categorize. She knew how messy, how artificial the self was, as well as the difficulty of becoming someone of our own choosing.

I couldn't think of what else to say, so I stood, and she did too.

We walked in a drifting fashion into the lobby.

"Would you like to come up?" I asked.

She didn't look at me, just nodded, and took my hand, interlacing her fingers in mine.

In the elevator, we kissed. I drew back and touched her cheek with my thumb.

"Are you okay?"

"Does my persona not seem okay?" she asked and a slight wry smile came onto her lips.

The elevator doors lurched open, and we walked together now, my arm around her waist. We separated briefly so I could unlock the door.

I left the light off. We kissed. She kicked off her shoes, and I did the same. Then we lay on the bed, on our sides, face to face, and just felt each other breathe. She reached up for a kiss, closed her eyes and exhaled. She was touching my face, tracing around my ear, and then exploring my temple and hair, gliding her fingertips along the lines of my skull. The sensation, the pleasure, felt closer to me than my thoughts.

I was suddenly intensely drowsy, and my breathing involuntarily deepened.

"I just need to close my eyes," I said. "I'm sorry."

"You don't have to apologize."

She drew closer, her hand now on the back of my neck.

"When I studied anthropology," she said, "I found myself blocked. I couldn't interview people or make them subjects, because then they responded as subjects. They were aware of my expectation of story and its reception, and that caused them to produce a text of sorts, geared toward what I wanted. I couldn't tell if they were showing me who they were or reflecting back my projections. But if I just sat with them and partook of their lives, I felt something of who they were. It was hard to make a story of that or convince academic advisers of what my experience meant. It was just a human feeling of being alive next to another person. I like silence for that reason. I like what you said about stillness. If I'm quiet enough, I can sense the realities around me."

I was grateful to listen—that she hadn't wanted to make love right away. I generally liked to lie and talk and relax before sex, to reset—and even then I preferred the lovemaking to be gradual. I rarely enjoyed veering into that need, or the sudden theatrics, the jockeyed intercourse—frantic ministrations and sexual provocations, galloping toward climax.

My brain had dominated my life—extracting an intellectual toll for every visceral experience it allowed the animal to have—and sometimes it locked me into a perception or way of thinking so strongly that, only after a brief nap, could I disconnect from it and wake capable of being present.

My eyes seemed to close with greater weight. I suddenly had the impression of stepping on ice and slipping. I gave a jerk. Her fingers were still in my hair and I shut my eyelids against the dark, and then I was waking and we were kissing. We undressed each other, touching, leaving space and time for each other's fingertips. She slid on top of me, and we made love, gradually, patiently, waking into it.

I was grateful for these vanishing intersections, her body adding and erasing dimensions of myself—to touch and hold the sensation of the touching in a fluid continuity with a past that was being released. We are these clusters of expectation, spiraling away, galaxies, and then these miraculous crossings.

When I woke again, it was once more from a dream of the misted river. I blinked in the dark, unable to see Sola. The air was somewhat warm and humid but not unpleasant, and I eased slowly onto my side.

She was sitting on the edge of the bed, in a posture like meditation—her chest lightly lifted, her shoulders back, her waist long. In the florid glow of the digital clock, her spine was a long, faint curve of shadow.

I shifted on the mattress, deliberately, so that my touch wouldn't surprise her. I reached and slowly traced the line of her back, descending by degrees, first with one fingertip, and then two, and soon all of them, until my hand came to rest on the small bend of her lumbar.

She didn't move, and I rolled closer, slipping my arm around her waist, my forearm resting on her thighs and my mouth to her hip.

I lay like that, my eyes closed as I sensed the slight shifts of her breathing, until I fell back asleep.

8

THE KING OF THE SMUGGLERS

I woke into the dream. Mist filled the hotel room. Sola lay on her side, facing away. Beyond the walls, the city's rumble was the river's. I gripped the edge of the mattress. My father had been dead for nearly twenty years, but I sensed him about to materialize from the granular mist—his dark hair, his gaze, his faintly olive skin.

I shut my eyes. I didn't want Sola to wake into this dream. The sound of the river grew louder, the way my breathing and heartbeat had during childhood night terrors, when the room reverberated violently with a nameless hum that might have been silence's totality, or the very movement of the blood thrumming in my veins.

My father had been an absence, working on scattered business projects, and later, when I was ten, my mother fled with me to the United States. Only after five years did I see him again, when I returned to Vancouver.

Memories of that time are unlike anything else I have lived: raw impressions of the world when I was so uncertain, so torn from moorings as I verged on homelessness, that I felt emotionless, like a parched skin walking through cold mist.

I might have slipped back into sleep. I opened my eyes and the room was normal. The antimalarial—Pentus—had to be altering my dreams. I'd read blogs by those who'd lost their minds after taking it, except they'd sounded so naturally predisposed to drama that I'd considered their lunacy a preexisting condition. Yet I knew it was a failure of the imagination to think oneself exempt from madness.

Later, Sola and I agreed that the best way to search for the girl would be independently, in separate cars, and that we'd call each other if we saw her or learned anything.

After she'd left, Oméga rang my cell, and I told him I was on my way down, again acutely aware of his generosity.

As soon as I got in the Land Rover, it pulled into the street, captained by Oméga's laconic driver—a muscled man with a knob of belly as perfectly curved as a swallowed basketball, on which he rested a palm whenever the traffic slowed.

As usual, Oméga and I sat in the back. The blue threads of his shirt were run through with gold, and he again touched the button near its collar often, just above his scar, as if the fidget were a defensive motion, a belated desire to protect the place where he'd been wounded.

"The dwarf," he said, "he goes by different names. Some people call him Napoléon. Some call him Vladimir."

"Vladimir?" I asked, trying to mute the shock in my voice.

Oméga glanced over at me, seeming somewhat surprised at my reaction.

"It's no big deal," he said. "The Congo has traditional respect for *mokonzi*. We admire powerful men. We call illegal gas sellers in the streets Kaddafis, and when Saddam Hussein was executed, I remember people shaking their heads and saying, 'Such a powerful man.' It was as if an ancient tree had been felled. And there was of course Mobutu, our homegrown *mokonzi*. We understand how power changes us and how much a great man can accomplish. This is why Americans confuse us, acting like frustrated children who need help and then, all of a sudden, like tyrants, and then like children again, blaming others for their problems."

"Maybe," I said, "we don't fully assume our power because we can't see it."

He shrugged. "To us, an American's power is evident, until he throws a tantrum and shows he is a pretender with a heavy pocketbook. Anyway, the dwarf sometimes goes by Vladimir or simply Putin, but more often Napoléon or just Léon."

The Land Rover had left the downtown. The wheels thudded off the broken pavement into a road little more than a dusty gully. The shanties were cobbled together—scraps of wood, metal, and plastic filmed with red dust—so monochrome I had the impression that we'd driven into the frames of a sepia past.

After a long lane, we pulled into an enclosure with a concrete wall, where the king of the smugglers waited in the doorway of a house that, though low, was the nicest in the neighborhood. He stood shirtless, his pant waist held with a thick leather belt, his body as small as a child's, as gnarled as that of a retiring wrestler, but with a head like the bust of Socrates.

"Napoléon," he introduced himself with the hard shake of a muscular hand and stared into my eyes. He fully owned the power of his small body—had taken stock of what he possessed and become it—to great effect.

He led us inside, where we sat on comfortable reclining chairs cut from bamboo, the concrete around us radiating cool.

A teenage girl with cornrows and blue-tattooed ankles brought out a large plastic bottle of Coke and poured it into cups.

A negotiation ensued between Oméga and Napoléon in Lingala. Oméga spoke at length, moving his hand, before Napoléon replied just as copiously.

Maybe an impression from the previous night's dream had returned, but something about the powerful man reminded me of my father, who, though by no means a little person, had been fairly small, asserting dominance despite his limitations. Or maybe they spoke similarly: the deliberate, muscular working of the jaw, the clout of each word on lips that pulled and clutched against the teeth.

Even toward the end of Napoléon's discourse, when he moved his hand side to side, indicating uncertainty or difficulty, he did so as if casting something off—shrugging his knotted shoulders with indifference—clearly conveying that the money wasn't worth the trouble or effort of attaining what Oméga wanted.

The discussion shifted to clear negotiation, each taking turns asking and the other avowing, until I had a sense—from the slowly affirming motions of their heads—that a deal had been made.

"*Les hommes blancs*," Napoléon said to me in French, hardly missing a beat, "white men, there are so many, you see, and I don't know all their names. Not their true names. John or Pierre or Karl or Hans. They come and ask me to make things happen, and I do. They come from all over the world to be cowboys here. To sell cars that are illegal to sell in their countries. Cars that were caught in floods. Cars in which people were murdered. Stolen cars. Or to make porn films with teenage girls. Or to get drugs. They come to me because they know that my word is good. If people hear that I am selling knowledge to any white man who can afford it, then what will happen to everything I have built? I have cripples delivering drugs. I have dwarves going across the river every day to Brazzaville, terrifying the customs inspectors into submission. So helping you is not easy, but you are lucky, because Monsieur Richmond has made enemies who are looking for him. There is a man named Vladimir. You go to your hotel and ask at the bar. Ask at the bar at any of the big hotels or restaurants, and people will know him. But ask quietly, since he does not like attention."

I was confused, having been certain—based on the information Oméga had given me—that the man who'd mentioned Vladimir in the hotel restaurant had simply been referring to Napoléon by another nickname. But now it seemed that there were two Vladimirs, and I had been alerted to the other one entirely by accident. My head reeled with the convulsive sense of time looping, and I tried to remember whether a man had actually come to my table and stood at my back as if to assassinate me. I had the paper with Vladimir's number. I pressed my fingertips to my pocket to feel its crepitation.

"And as for the girl," Napoléon told me, "if you need help finding her, then you're not looking hard enough."

"What should I do?"

"Don't try to find her yourself. You'll scare her."

“Why?”

“Because you’re white.”

“Isn’t she white?” I asked, only because I was curious to hear whether he saw her as such.

He just shrugged.

“Men pay a lot for her,” he said. “They send people to me and I send boys to find her and they tell her. It would be sad to have her off the street. But as a favor to the pastor, I will tell you what you should already know.”

“Yes?”

“Find a pimp and ask him to get you a white girl, and she’ll be the one.”

9

THE TRUE NAME OF PASTOR OMÉGA

The ride into the shantytown had been so long—the traffic bad and now much worse—that by the time we pulled into the restaurant, it was well into the afternoon and we weren't sure if we were having lunch or dinner but were both famished and surly. Oméga excused himself to the bathroom.

I called the number I'd received the previous evening at dinner, and, after one ring, a man with a Slavic accent answered with a greeting I didn't recognize.

"I got your number from—"

"I know," he said. "What time you want?"

"When's the—"

"Hotel," he said with a heavily aspirated *H*. "Tonight. At the bar."

He hung up.

Oméga returned, smiling his smile that was now familiar. When we'd first met, I'd foolishly let myself be blinded by a lifetime of films portraying the jollity of hackneyed good-hearted Africans. And though he did often laugh as a first response—before his eyes became serious and studious—I'd begun to wonder if the laugh was a smoke screen, or simply a different way of laughing from those I knew—a visceral acknowledgment that absorbed the shock of life's absurdity and allowed his humanity to express itself in the face of existence's maddening onslaught, before he decided how to deal with it.

The restaurant was largely empty, and we found seats just outside, at a plastic table beneath a beer umbrella. The dish of the day was chicken baked in aluminum foil. I ordered a Fanta, he a Primus. Within a minute, he was halfway through the bottle and then slowed, sighing, finally appearing to savor it.

He took his phone from his pocket and opened Maps.

"It's time we consider the path of your journey," he said and shifted the image to the country's center, over which the Congo river sketched its arc. "This is where Hew has his camp, in Maniema, near the confluence of these rivers. But right now he is in the east, making a park in the mountains where Terra worked. You will need to go there first. I will help you get travel papers and journalist documents, so you won't be harassed along the way."

His thumb came to rest on the dark green of mountains in North Kivu province, near Rwanda, and in his extended silence and the gravity with which he looked at the satellite image dissected with lines, I again sensed a shift in his mood.

"My family," he said but then just sat there, before blinking a few times and smiling—"my family is from the east, from North Kivu. I suppose I haven't told you much about that."

"No, you haven't," I said, not entirely sure what *that* referred to.

He continued staring at the phone's narrow window on the landscape before darkening its screen and putting it in his pocket.

"I had a normal childhood," he said. "A splendid childhood. The sunrises over the Virunga Mountains. The mist dissolving as the farm work begins. I thought everyone on earth had seen everything I had since the beginning of time. My father farmed the land. He had some cows and other animals, and I was the best student at the Catholic school. It was the sort of childhood in which you live thinking that the world is unchanging."

The waiter, a thin, stooped man in a too-large white shirt as slack as an inpatient's gown, came out, paced slowly past and stood on the gravel, close enough to listen. Oméga paused, giving him a long, bothered look. The waiter glanced over, turned, and hurried back inside.

"And then," Oméga said, "then there was the genocide in Rwanda, and the Tutsi invaded their homeland and forced out those who had massacred their kin. An entire nation of Hutu murderers and soldiers—and I suppose also many of those who were innocent enough—moved into the Congo, and the extermination of the Tutsis began here.

"My family was mixed, but we weren't too worried. I stayed in college until it nearly ceased to function, and to survive, I joined the Congolese army before our commander sold our weapons to the Rwandans. I threw away my uniform that night and left, and the next day the Rwandans and the rebels killed the soldiers with their own weapons—the very ones they'd sold the day before. I understood that with the help of the Rwandans the rebels would take over the Congo. So I joined them and walked across this land in the final weeks it was called Zaire, not really fighting, because the country was rotten then, and its defenses collapsed with each of our advances, and many of our enemies joined us.

"As we neared Kinshasa, Mobutu fled. We took the capital, and not long after, the next war broke out, when the new government expelled the Rwandans who'd helped them seize power. The Rwandans controlled and pillaged the east. I fought them this time, not out of any natural animosity, but simply because I didn't believe their motives were sound. They were in the Congo for the same reason that the Belgians and every world power have been here—for the minerals, the gold, the copper, the diamonds, the coltan. The country split apart, and it was years before I could finally return to my family's homestead. When I did, they were gone. The farm was weeds. The house was a shell.

"Standing in it, I was a boy again. Yes, I had fought in two wars, but in my father's house, I was a boy, waiting for my parents. And then a white man appeared—I can hardly remember from where—with a rifle. We stood there in that room with its blown-out window. At first, there was no indication he intended to kill me but for the way time slowed. I expected a flicker of hesitation, some trace of decision in his face, or the gathering determination to take a human life. But there was none of that. He stepped forward, almost mechanically, and he thrust his bayonet, as if he had no more bullets or didn't want to waste those that remained."

Oméga touched his chest, just below his throat.

"It caught me here," he said. "I don't know how I moved, but I moved with the blade. It seemed so deliberate, lingering beneath my skin, contemplating my depths, realizing that, despite my skin, I was human, and then committing itself to all it would take from me. I twisted and felt myself riding that edge, accepting it within me but following its motion so that it seemed part of me, as if we were on the same journey. Time was as slow as the final heartbeats before death. That is how I know I died. I saw a new life and gave the old one to the blade. I grew into the new man I would become, moving into the world, guiding my body off the knife."

He picked up the large brown bottle of Primus and tipped more beer into his glass. From the information he'd shared about his life, I realized that we were nearly the same age, though he seemed much older—not just more self-confident but more affirmed in his existence.

"There were many mercenaries here, from many countries," he told me. "The war was never quite over, and I had gone into a bad area not as a soldier but as a civilian, to find my family. That's why I was in the house. In each one, everything had been stripped out—the electrical wires and light sockets, the glass in the windows. The mercenaries took better things. I don't know where this one was from. I didn't search his body. His eyes were blue, almost as clear as yours."

The waiter came out with two plates of chicken, placed them before us, and hastened back inside, hunched within his flapping shirt.

"The name my father chose for me," Oméga said, "was Duma. It means 'cheetah' in Swahili. In his youth, before buying the farm, he traveled for work and met an impressively strong and business-savvy man with this name, and so he chose it for me. But I felt a natural gravity toward the Bible, and what was a cheetah but a simple animal of God's creation—not a spiritual man but a predator? On the plane, what I did not tell you was that my childhood nickname was Oméga, since I was the last of my mother's children and was very determined and willful in nature. She would make a joke, quoting from Revelation, saying, 'I am the Alpha and the Omega, the beginning and the ending.' And then she would tell me, 'Oméga, you are the last one. We used up all of our energy making you, and it shows.'

"What I also didn't tell you was that when I picked up the copy of Rimbaud's poems from the floor of the house, that was my house. It was my book, in the room of my childhood, and I read that poem and I saw the violet light of the creator's eyes, so glorious, and yet, maybe not so different from the eyes of the man who'd tried to kill me. And I knew that he hadn't been a man, not entirely, at least not any more than any of us are men to each other but rather the motions of divine or devilish hands halting us or striking us toward our final judgment. I thought of my earthly parents and the loving way they called me Oméga, and in those days, when I could not find my way out of that house or the land around it, when I slept in the forest, I asked who I was, Duma or Oméga—the predator or the *prophète.* This might seem a theoretical question, but I have known the horror of the predator and I have known the loneliness of the *prophète*. And so now, when so many worldly callings come to me each day, asking me to take up the reins in my country and to fight for it again, in less violent but equally committed ways, I ask myself the question of my name and consider whether I can serve this Congo and still stay true to God."

Oméga sighed and emptied his glass, and then looked at my eyes.

"I hate this about you Westerners," he said.

"What?" I asked, startled but trying to hide it.

"If you were speaking with a Catholic nun or a Buddhist monk who was asking the same questions about the demands of their faith and its loneliness, your expression would be filled with sympathy and perhaps awe."

"And with what is my expression filled?"

"Pity for the superstitious savage."

I stammered, trying to find words but my brain was too busy examining myself, attempting to decide if my face had shown that of which he'd accused me.

I had the impression that something else was happening between us but that I wasn't able to think fast enough—as if we were boxing not just with words but with glances and expressions, with the very presence and energy of our bodies.

My jumbled sentence that came out made no sense, at once apology and denial, but he waved his hand and pointed at my plate.

"Eat your chicken," he told me. "As far as white men go, you are not terrible."

10

VLADIMIR DOESN'T LIKE TO WAIT (ENTER ALTON HOOKE)

Even as I disembarked from the Land Rover and thanked Oméga, I felt outwitted—though in what, I wasn't sure. Alone in the hotel parking lot, I took a moment to catch my breath before my next meeting, walking a few paces in the cooling dark beneath a well-kempt palm. I felt strangely pleased to be revealed to myself—that Oméga might have seen a judgment in my face whose presence I hadn't suspected. Traveling, I sometimes felt I was drifting, fleeing things of which I was never quite sure, and yet there were moments of encountering myself on the road.

Of course, I did regret that I might have looked at Oméga the way he described. After my mother fled my father, taking me with her to rural Virginia, I struggled to make sense of the barriers between whites and blacks. Black gazes struck me as guarded, with what I perceived as wariness, weariness, and pain, but also endurance, resistance, defiance, and rage. Whites seemed to look at blacks with condescension, hate and fear, or not at all; or with discomfort and guilt, which also became a way of not seeing, if not a reason not to. There was rarely an open meeting of the eyes that allowed the space to discover who the other person was.

Living in the Congo for the first time, I'd felt relieved that the gaze was easier, despite the barriers. I'd believed there was something purifying, even healing, about those exchanges. Only now I wondered whether there were codes here that I didn't know how to read and had failed even to notice—or whether my gaze itself was contaminated with judgment I couldn't identify. And in truth, I hadn't put much stock in Oméga's story, though his family had been murdered—and he'd nearly been murdered himself—and though the desire for a redemption of the spirit made sense. But I generally considered stories of spiritual awakening to be set pieces, shared less for their truth than their impact on the listener. (He was a preacher after all.) Even if I was unconvinced that I'd empathize with nuns or monks, I was grateful for the window into myself to evaluate any superiority or disdain I might harbor.

I leaned my head back and sighed. A few stars pocked the amber sky, the humidity gathering the city's tungsten emission. An incoming airliner passed low, hovering in the distance with an avian quality, as if it had just spread its wings against the cushion of air.

It was time for my next encounter. I walked through the hotel's sliding doors and then into its restaurant, nerving myself for duplicity and danger.

I took stock of the men at the bar who might comfortably wear the name Vladimir, and the one who seemed most likely—seated at the far end—was the one whose cell phone, when I dialed the number on the paper, rang. He picked it up off the bar, looked at the screen and refused the call. I walked over and took the seat next to him, and he tilted his head to examine me.

His receding, carefully combed blond hair decorated the sort of mug I'd expected—a thin nose and bony jaw freshly scraped with a razor—but he had a yellow malarial complexion, and the blue of his eyes was faintly glaucous, as if they'd steamed up from within. He appeared enswathed in his suit jacket, so painfully thin that I wondered if he wore it to warm himself against the blast of the restaurant's air conditioning, or simply for appearances.

"I don't like to wait," he grumbled.

"I'm sorry," I said, trying to recall if we'd picked a time.

"I don't trust people who say sorry."

"Oh. Okay," I replied in an effort not to apologize again.

"You are looking for me?"

"I heard you might be able to help."

"Go. Tell me."

"I'm looking for information about a man named Richmond Hew."

He'd been facing forward but now looked at me more directly. I'd considered that Vladimir might be a nickname because of a resemblance in image or spirit to Putin, but seeing him more clearly, I suspected it was just his name.

"I know this man," he said. "I have much information on him, but I cannot see why I give you this. It will not help me."

His hands rested on the bar and he turned up one of his palms, showing his emaciated wrist, its spidery tendons and veins.

"I'm not sure either," I told him.

"You are what? World-saver? Mercenary? Investigator?"

"Journalist," I said, and he laughed, shaking his head, and repeated, "Jour-na-list," as if it were the most pointless occupation in existence.

"So what you want?" he continued. "Reveal his corruption? Tell a good story, exciting story, like a movie, but in newspaper?"

"That's about right."

"Okay then. I offer you deal. Take it, and we work together. Don't take it, and you go. I am sitting too long. My ass hurts. I don't like to wait."

"What's the deal?"

"Richmond Hew, he steal something from me. He want me to believe someone else steal it, but I know. He blame it all on Alton Hooke—"

"Pardon me. On whom?"

"Alton Hooke. American. He pretend he is ex-military. I am ex-military. I can tell he is not. He is finance guy who shoots guns in the forest on weekends. Pathetic. But he come to me to make me deal. I do not know where he met you."

"Me?" I said. "I don't know anyone named Alton Hooke."

Vladimir shushed me, as if someone else in the restaurant might hear. He narrowed his eyes and enunciated a long *H*, saying, "Hew. Where he met Hew."

"Right. Of course. I'm sorry."

"Don't apologize. You kill my trust."

I just nodded this time, and he continued with a story about smuggling during the war in the Congo, and how the borders became porous, with every man trying to get minerals out. Right before the war ended, a group of Serbian mercenaries had been attempting to sell a huge cache of diamonds to Rwandan soldiers, when their region was overrun by government forces. A long string of betrayals and atrocities followed, and each time he said that someone was killed, he shaped his hand into a gun and said, "Klink."

"Eventually all of them dead." He snapped his thumb down repeatedly. "Klink, klink, klink."

The diamond cache was hidden and abandoned in the rainforest, and now, nearly ten years later, Hooke contacted Vladimir, looking for someone to help him get the diamonds out of the country.

"You see, most smuggling happen in the east," Vladimir explained, "but the Rwandans and Ugandans control it and pay shit. For a man to make good money, he need to get the diamonds out on his own. This is why they ask me."

Though he didn't say it, I gathered that this was the nature of his connection with Napoléon, and that Napoléon had planned on making a profit on this exchange as well, hence his reason for directing me to Vladimir, though someone else had previously done so for reasons I didn't understand, or by accident.

"And what does all this have to do with Hew?"

"Hew," he said in a low voice, driving his gaze into mine, as if telling me to speak more quietly, "he is in the forest for years. He find out about the diamonds from his people."

"His people?"

"The forest people. The black people." He gestured in a faintly circular motion, indicating the world around us. "He knew that warlords would take the diamonds. It would be hard to get them out. Everything is searched at every stop in Congo, and warlords would take them. Where Hooke come from, I don't know. But he found me. I don't know how. He ask people."

"Where is he now?"

"That's the problem. Hooke is disappeared. Probably dead. Klink! I send man to talk to Hew. Hew tell him that Hooke has the diamonds, and Hooke—paf!—gone. But he also has some of the money for the diamonds. Also gone."

He repeated "Paf!" and gestured, turning his palm up and opening his fingers quickly, somewhat explosively, like a puff of smoke, it seemed.

I understood now. Hew had demanded a partial payment first, for the sake of safety, and Vladimir had been planning on making much more once he sold the diamonds. He'd paid Hooke, and Hooke had gone into the forest and disappeared.

"You will just need to find Alton Hooke's information. He is blubber mouth."

"A blabbermouth?"

"Yes, blubber, blubber. He say everything in e-mails, text messages. I forward them to you after you get me the diamonds. Then you can tell this story about the diamonds. Vladimir is not my true name, so nothing will change. Please make me a good character. Not so skinny please. I have been sick. I will be much stronger soon. I have always been a strong man."

The conversation appeared to be coming to an end, and I wasn't sure what this lead could do for me other than send me across the Congo, asking people if they'd seen a white man named Alton Hooke.

"By any chance," I asked in a hushed voice, "have you heard anything about Richmond Hew—about his interest in little girls?"

"How do I know what he does on his free time?"

"I mean, I thought you might have—"

"What is little girl? Like baby?"

"No, like twelve or thirteen . . ."

His eyebrows gave a slight, baffled jerk, and he moved his skeletal hand indifferently.

"We have deal. You have my number."

I stood but hesitated. I had nothing to lose by asking one last question.

"Do you know where I can find a pimp?"

"Ha, journalist, okay. This is easy."

"I've heard there's a white girl living in the streets. She's a prostitute."

"Ah, so this is not for fucking. For business. You are boring man."

I caught myself before I said sorry.

"I can pay the pimp," I told him, "if he can help me find her."

Vladimir drew a thin notepad from his jacket and copied three numbers from his phone's contacts and tore the page off.

"Just so you know, everyone here is pimp." He motioned about. "Bartender pimp, reception pimp, guy who sweeps floor pimp. But for white girl, you want big pimp. These are big pimp numbers."

Back in my room, I went online, and the trove of information on Alton Hooke stunned me. He curated—until a month ago—a sprawling blog called "American Rogue." His bio photo showed him in desert camo holding an AK-47: tall, blond, blue eyed, with the jaw of a WASP patriarch, though youthful, in his late twenties or early thirties.

The text read like a mission statement.

After five years killing it in finance, pillaging Wall Street, I'm moving on to become the next American incarnation of the writer-adventurer—a cold fusion of Jack London, Hemingway, Kerouac, and Cormac McCarthy, only better, truly on the edge

The style in the blog posts was baroque, whether describing the extreme sports—usually the sorts of obstacle courses currently enjoying popularity among young men who held office jobs—or shooting friends with paintballs in the Mojave, or trekking through the Rockies on a survivalist training.

I'm American Psycho meets Daniel Boone, with a dash of Wolverine.

He'd probably believed he could fool everyone with the diamonds and money, but judging from how he wrote, I suspected his bones were tattooed deep in the jungle's loam.

I skimmed his blogs with an eye to lines I could quote—for those glinting fragments of persona that I could best assemble into a character of my own.

I should've gone to war. I've suffered over this—worse than the usual civilian guilt. I was a born conduit for adrenaline, designed for climax. But I had no affinity for command structures, strutting superiors, the constant waiting, the guarding of civilian projects in boring places, or the endless sitting in a metal box rumbling along a malevolent highway, soon to be barbecued by insurgent explosives.

I opened a new tab and typed "Alton Hooke Congo." A dead link came up to a three-month-old post on his blog. The entry had been deleted, but I found the text cached, on a website that crawled the web. It appeared that Hooke had signed up for a low budget ecotour led by an ex-Navy SEAL, who took small groups through the rainforest.

His blog openly discussed diamonds, the text a rambling breakdown of financial figures concerning their value on the open market, intermixed with the casualty figures for the Congo Wars pulled from Wikipedia (I cross-referenced): 250,000 to 800,000 dead in the first war (and 222,000 refugees missing), as many as 5.4 million dead in the second.

This was followed by fantasies of what might go wrong.

> *Starvation? Cannibalism? Would I go native, wear the local talismans, douse my body in holy oil and run naked into battle, believing I'm impervious to bullets? Take five wives? Build a palace in the rainforest? Trade in chattel, human or otherwise? That's the thing with chaos. At least it offers the sort of freedom America was built on.*

I went back to other posts in his blog and continued to skim. In one entry, he claimed to be descended from John Hooke, a Mayflower pilgrim.

This caused my brain some mild consternation. Though the detail didn't actually matter, it unsettled me, since I knew that I would include it in my exposé.

Journalists use such particulars to create contrast and texture, but what I would really be implying is that we don't expect the descendants of America's white forefathers (many of whom advertised sterling genocidal credentials) to become swindling, murderous maniacs. And yet the fact that one of these blue-blooded psychopaths had lost his way in the heart of the Congo would do wonders for my story.

Maybe it wasn't unreasonable to think about film rights after all. I had a faceless hebephiliac psychopath three decades in the jungle, a sexy ecowarrior with autocratic tendencies, and now Hooke—the wannabe cowboy, the perfect faux-gothic comedic touch, though treacherous nonetheless. Yet another Kurtz.

II

THE NARRATIVE GENEALOGY OF A DEMON

As I was reading Hooke's blog, Sola texted to ask if she could come over. I said yes and intended to stay up until she arrived, but after half an hour, I dozed on the couch, dreaming like a pugilist, it seemed, because when she knocked, my jaw ached and the muscles of my neck were clenched. I recalled only glimpses—flying in a Cessna over the rainforest ten years before, circling a pillar of smoke that had once been a village, the shapes of fallen bodies easily visible from the sky, silhouetted by the dark patches of earth around them—the entire scene sufficiently two-dimensional for my brain to accept it.

"I told Bram," Sola said and kissed me. "Are you all right?"

"Yes. I'm fine. I just dozed off. What did you tell Bram?"

There had also been a dream segment with my father, again, and I was concerned that a man who'd been dead twenty years and of whom I almost never dreamt was suddenly haunting my sleep.

"Are you listening?" Sola asked, and I realized she'd been speaking.

"Sorry. I'm a little groggy."

"I told Bram about us."

"How did he take it?"

She shrugged. "The thing I had with him has been over for a while. He kept trying to blame you, but I told him that I hadn't known of your existence until recently. I'm perfectly capable of making bad decisions and having sexual adventures on my own terms."

I cleared my throat. "Bad decisions?" I asked.

"I guess I have a weakness for a certain sort of man."

She placed her palms on my cheeks and kissed me, and then looked into my eyes as I wondered if she was comparing me to Rees.

"I think we need to get you to bed."

"I'm sorry. I'm feeling a little out of it."

She began unbuttoning her blouse. "Mind if I take a quick shower?"

"Not at all." I lay back down, and she spoke from the bathroom, over the clatter of water on the tiles.

"I called several embassies, and they've contacted the police. This should prevent them from trying to sell the girl to Bram again. And regardless, he has to return to Amsterdam. His flight is tomorrow. He's anxious about your article, so don't be surprised if he shows up in the morning and pressures you into interviewing him."

"I was planning on doing that anyway, and tomorrow works fine."

"Any leads on the girl?"

"I've been told I should just call the big-time pimps."

"Have you?"

"I was planning on doing it in the morning."

"I don't think pimps are known for being morning people."

"Good point. I'll do it now while you're in the shower."

She thanked me and eased the bathroom door nearly closed.

I dialed the three phone numbers and spoke in French to men with gruff voices who repeated my request—"Une fille *mundele*?"

"Oui, c'est ça. Une fille blanche. Europénne. Elle a onze ou douze ans."

Two said they knew of her and would track her down. The third pimp proposed getting me an albino, but I insisted on what I was looking for and he said, "An albino, it's almost the same thing," and I said, "No thank you, but please call me if you hear about a white girl."

Speaking to the pimps had fully awakened me, and by the time Sola slipped into bed, I had a heightened sense of the fragrances of soap and shampoo. But as I moved my hands over her skin, I also felt reluctant, as if my brief connection to those men had somehow dirtied me.

"Any luck?" she asked between kisses.

"I've left my cell on. If it rings tonight, that's why."

In the dark, Sola and I talked for a while of other things. I told her about Hew and Terra and Hooke, and she described the work she was doing for an organization based here—"The usual," she said, "identifying cultural infrastructures to facilitate development projects."

At some point as we spoke, I closed my eyes for a little too long.

There is a deep sleep that comes for me not simply with physical contact but with a sort of natural intimacy and connection. It is often short-lived, the restfulness switching to restlessness, because—I have come to believe—the other person nudges me toward conventionality, distancing me from how I've learned to exist.

Tonight, the restfulness lasted until sometime before dawn, when the dreams began, and I woke from the mist and river again, from the fear that my father would appear. I was thinking about the girl and what I was doing here, and of convictions. Like some self-appointed self-actualization guru, I could hardly speak without bringing up convictions, yet mine flitted beyond my field of vision—a rare creature that I knew existed but had never seen.

When I dropped back into sleep, a pair of dark eyes hung before me, blazing with violet light, and I jolted awake with fear, though I didn't know why. I hadn't been threatened.

Sola sat on the bedside, facing away, her back lit by the glow of the usual hotel apparatuses.

My fingers wanted to touch it, but whose fingers were they? There was hardly a self, just old nodes, attachments to broken pieces of the past like scars in the nerves of my brain to which the mind couples in its confusion, the self floating inside a vast cognitive short circuit.

I thought of villains, enemies, purpose. My chronic cogitation churned inside my mind's stupidity until it beat out the connection that should have been obvious—qualities that my father shared with Hew. He'd been a criminal, building a life that appeared vaguely conventional from the outside, while torturing its inhabitants on the inside, and then destroying it all, releasing himself toward his next incarnation. There had been a girl in his story too.

When I woke again, from yet another river (this one narrow, fast, with rapids, edged with ice) and dark gravel roads over which the sky faded out through naked branches—Sola was lying on the couch.

"You thrashed in your sleep," she said when I crouched next to her and kissed her cheek.

"I'm sorry."

"I tried rubbing your back."

"Thank you."

She had an unmistakable look of regret, as if she'd realized that she'd exchanged one crazy man for another. Perhaps she hadn't been meditating after all, just sitting on the bedside, trying to decide what to do.

By the time she left to continue looking for the girl, I'd received an e-mail from an editor at *GQ* saying he wanted the story about the white demon, the girl, and the mad Dutch anthropologist.

I'd already begun writing up the piece, and I spent some time on it that morning, before taking a break to book a flight to Goma for the next day, to North Kivu province, where Terra had worked.

The hotel phone rang. It was the receptionist, telling me that a Monsieur Bram was in the lobby.

As I stepped out of the elevator, I briefly felt that I was seeing the older Bram. A compound of harsh emotions had corrugated his skin, though not quite erasing the red-freckled circles on his cheeks.

He shook my hand. "I have to go to the airport soon, but I really should be quoted at length about my study on the girl."

"I wouldn't have it any other way."

"I also brought a more precise contract regarding the film rights."

We sat in armchairs near the window, and as I read the contract, he couldn't help but talk.

"I should be quoted on the mix of African beliefs and Pentecostal values. This is an area where I have blazed trails. You see, American Pentecostal missionaries brought the idea of spiritual warfare here. Congolese pastors interpreted this idea through the lens of Bantu ceremonies in which the people appeal to the spirits that are both the source of bounty and of suffering. These spirits originally maintained harmony in nature. A woman who took more fruit from the communal forest could be identified by the withering of her child's leg. A hunter who greedily killed more antelopes than the others would be revealed when his wife miscarried. Now, though, these spirits—the guardians of harmony—are demons, and if they offer bounty, it's a trick that leads to suffering. The only safe bounty comes from God, and the prophet guides his flock by discerning between the harmful seductions of the demons and the true rewards of faith."

"I see," I said, having paused him long enough to turn my voice recorder on. "And is it common for street children to be accused of being demons?"

"Yes. Very."

"And do many of them believe it's true?"

"Most do. They are children after all. Just as we believed in Santa when adults told us he was real, they are being told by parents and preachers that they are demons. But while most believe it, only a few truly own it. Their possession becomes a source of power, of resistance, actually, to the society that marginalizes them. They see the terror it creates in adults, and they use that terror for protection. They repeat the stories of demons to each other and, as a result, their beliefs thrive.

"This is the source of the duality in the girl's narrative.

She needs the demon's power and embodies it as a witch, and yet she flees it, knowing that being a demon is what alienates and destroys her. Even her senses of temporality and identity are discontinuous. She is both white and black. Her life begins each time the demon possesses her, and yet she is also engaged in a long struggle against him."

Listening, I reclined in the cushioned chair, and what ensued could hardly be called an interview so much as a lecture designed to imprint ownership on a subject and establish prestige.

"I have come to the conclusion," Bram said, "that, by analyzing the narrative structure of her story, I can identify her origins. I'm calling her Luna, by the way, to facilitate the research, though she never gave a name. As I was saying, her story has Western undertones, and by Western, I mean Wild West. I sense something of the frontier—cowboys and Indians, as well as the American courage to go into the unknown. She has an obsession with guns that's unusual in the Congo, and there are strange renderings in Lingala that might actually translate into '*The Lone Ranger*' and '*The Wild Bunch*.'"

"Those aren't exactly references with which I'd expect someone of her generation to be familiar," I told him.

"No, but they are part of the American heritage. Imagine a girl watching late night TV while her mother is out working. Or maybe her father likes those movies. I have also identified narrative signatures quite similar, in her stories of demons and nightly excursions, to *Where the Wild Things Are*."

I had to admit to myself that what he'd just said was indeed a juicy detail for the article, so I refrained from interrupting again, though I remained skeptical.

As he struggled to create a genealogy for her whiteness,

he became more voluble, lifting a finger, spinning it, prodding the air. I could see that he already fancied himself a luminary of the anthropological world, the grand nabob of risky colonial fieldwork.

Only when he was clearly winding down did I ask some hard questions, inserting them into the conversation like jabs.

"So why did you keep her and not alert the embassies?"

His eyes widened with surprise, his camo-green irises small within the bloodshot whites.

"She came with no passport and no way to identify her nationality, and I saw no harm in speaking to her for a few days."

I didn't have time to consider the merit of his response before another question came to me.

"Did you see yourself as saving her?"

"Certainly. Only by understanding her story and her origins could I figure out how to help her."

"And did you not feel inclined to save her friends?"

"Her friends?"

"The street children she lives with."

"They are Congolese."

"So they do not need saving?"

His face slackened, his freckles going dim and rusty.

"Sola mentioned to me," he said, "that you have also been looking for the girl."

"Yes. I have."

"And have you not seen many other street children? The black ones?"

"Yes. I suppose so," I admitted, seeing where this was leading.

He gestured upstairs.

"Are they all relaxing now in your hotel room, raiding the minibar, ordering room service, and watching pay-per-view?"

"No."

"I see."

We stared at each other.

"Please," he said in a stark, guttural voice that suggested a deeper reserve of strength than I'd suspected, "do not ask me the holier-than-thou questions of the expat who believes he is better than the rest of us, who is somehow not colonial when the rest of us are. Anyone who has been through the most basic of academic formations knows that there is no story more colonial than that of the good white, so you may as well embrace your presence here because, no matter what you do, history—and especially the sorts of people with whom you hope to ally—will judge you harshly."

He placed his extended fingers on the arms of his chair, stood, and then reached out to shake my hand.

"I look forward to reading your work," he said. "Please do not hesitate to contact me for a follow-up interview."

He motioned to my copy of the contract that had his business card stapled to the top left corner, and then, from his bag, he took a new draft of the revised, translated interviews with the girl.

"Good luck with Sola," he added, and the way he raised his eyebrows struck me as distinctly foreign and suggestive, perhaps to convey that he'd seen through me or caught me out.

He turned away and walked toward the hotel exit with a quality that I have since come to see as a sort of Kurtzian fatality—his chest neither lifted nor collapsed, the set of his shoulders at once resigned and determined: the neutral, unquestioning stride of a white man who knows his place in history.

12

THE MURDER OF A CHILD

Back in Room 22(2), I kicked off my shoes, lay on the bed with the sheaf of papers, and picked up where I'd left off in the girl's story, though it seemed Bram had continued editing, further adapting the language.

> *Between headstones, we sit and make sure no demon is close. We dig a hole. We stick a branch in the ground next to it and each of us hang our* kapote.
>
> *At first, nothing happen. Those ugly sacs of man sap hang in the night. Then the moon shine in them. Inside the rubber, a light start up, like spark in dry grass, and it get brighter and brighter, like to blind us, and we watch the demon seed squirm inside. From every direction, through the graveyard, the spirits of the* mokonzi *appear, walking like on broken knees, arms out, like zombie—tripping, reaching . . .*

I paused, recalling that zombies were originally a Haitian social construct and wondering whether this might be Bram's insertion or a sign of the girl's American roots, though of course monster films had popularized the concept globally.

> *These spirits was pulled from the bodies of* mokonzi, *staggering toward the moonlit seed. When they walk past us, close enough to touch, we say Now! and drop the* kapote *in the hole, and the spirits fall in. They vanish like string of smoke.*
>
> *This how we kill the poison in the veins of the* mokonzi. *It how we kill the demon. Sometime* mokonzi *spirit go into hole and fizzle up. Sometime, if the demon the one who shoot the poison between my legs, it his spirit die, and I get my color back.*
>
> *The first time, I think it back forever. Me and Marvine and Keicha pat my arms and legs and laugh that I'm no longer* blanche. *But the demon he just die in the body he have here. We don't got much time to hide. He angry. He coming again over the ocean, riding on his knife, its blade pointed at my heart.*

I was annoyed by the editing, that Bram hadn't given me a copy of the original transcripts. For my article, I would have to play up his contrived character to explain this version of the story. Once the girl was found, I would interview her and use her testimony to create a more human character.

I skimmed the pages.

> Le démon blanc *jump between bodies, bleaching them out. He want me from inside and from outside. He use my body, but then I see him in the street, white face with life cooked out. Being me isn't enough. He must take*

me too. Make money with my body. Use my blood for kerosene and red wine. Drink from my skull, cook in it, wear it. Use my spine for TV antenna. Sleep in my hair, soft and warm. Watch through my eyes to see stars and planets, and then fly on through.

[. . .]

Sometime he ancient. Sometime he young. But he always white. White skin. White hair. White eyes.

[. . .]

Hurry up and do it to me. You may be demon, but you yuma, *you* mbakasa. *I destroy your soul and cure the color of my skin.*

[. . .]

My family is the children waiting for me in the street. We are all yanké. *They never stop waiting.*

[. . .]

We go to the cripples. They walk invisible. They are our friends.

[. . .]

I crossed the ocean on the blade of a knife.

That's what you say. You tell me you save me. You tell me you protect me but you trap me. Your face fat from eating babies and the hearts of the poor. But I am une socière. *I fly to Europe in the night and wear fur coats and diamonds. The wind carry my spirit to dance with jungle sorcerers. I kill you once. I do it again. Someday, I point my finger at you, like this, like gun, and that time you die forever.*

[. . .]

Rees: Who was your mother?

Luna: She fall in love with man and leave. She in the trees. In the mountains.

[. . .]

I never have mother. I a witch. I born from the sky.

[. . .]

Rees: What is your first memory, the oldest memory you have?

Luna: I cross the ocean on the blade of a knife.

Reading, I couldn't help but feel that the girl's words might yield a clue about Hew. But as soon as I lowered the pages and took a moment to consider this, I saw that the idea was absurd. I was doing what Bram had done—fitting her story into my own, an impulse so automatic, so natural feeling that I didn't even want to guard against it.

As for her mother, like many Westerners drawn to war—free spirits or bleeding hearts—she'd likely come to Kinshasa and died.

Lying on the hotel bed, staring at the unadorned square of ceiling, I rested the papers on my chest. Most of my own beliefs were no doubt invisible to me, and my conviction often seemed to be the importance of identifying them and divesting myself of their illusion of protection. But in favor of what? If not of openness to life, then at very least of the sort of self-invention that had taken over my social media newsfeed in recent years: articles on how to master mood, habits, and productivity, to hack every aspect of the self. Maybe these pursuits would be in favor not of openness but of emptiness—the senseless infinity of potential meaning and being, the nothingness beneath and around and within the reality over which we fret like bees cobbling together a hive.

My cell rang, and the self-reckoning that felt so unremitting blinked off.

It was Sola.

"Come meet me," she said, breathless. "We're in the market. The police are rounding up street children."

I grabbed my camera bag and ran out past the elevator to the stairs. In the parking lot, several taxi drivers were in the throes of a debate, one bringing his hand down as if striking the air with a hammer. He darted to his car before the others and intercepted me. I offered to pay extra if he drove fast, and as he swerved through the traffic, I readied my camera.

The market comprised rows of low shanties, patched together with boards, pieces of plastic and tin, and old political banners.

I called Sola just as she came into sight, walking quickly alongside a tall, lean police officer who kept swatting in her direction, motioning for her to go away. I hung up, found Oméga's number in my phone, and kept it on the screen.

"There were gunshots," she told me when I ran up next to her.

At the market's outskirts, as we rounded a concrete building—a warehouse of some sort, riddled with cracks—the officer spun around and held up his deeply lined palm, his fingers splayed out in warning.

Beyond him, two other policemen stood, looking down at a fallen child. The dust was already turning red.

Sola tried to push past him, and I lifted my camera, focused, and shot. The shutter clacked between each interval of zoom. The child's body framed by the two officers. The pointed face tucked into his own shoulder. The lips slightly parted on white teeth. The black boots and blue pant legs on either side.

The officer jerked the camera from my hands and shouted at me to get back, his face so close to mine that flecks of spittle struck my cheeks. He held up the camera as if to throw it or strike me with it.

Sola had taken the opportunity to run toward the child, but another of the policemen intercepted her, trying to hold her arms. From across the market, more officers were coming fast, abandoning their hunt, and I backed away.

The taxi I'd come in fled, reversing and then soaring out of the lot.

I hit send on my phone.

"Mon cher ami," Oméga said after a ring, and I stammered, telling him that the police were harassing us.

"Let me speak to their commander," he replied and I thrust the phone out.

This was a universal gesture of connection to a higher power, and all the police—seven of them now—stopped in place, one gripping Sola's arm and another with a rifle aimed at me.

The tall officer lowered the hand holding my camera and composed himself. He took the phone and said, "Oui." His yellow, malarial eyes gradually widened.

The silence was a cicada in my ear, the earth vague and spongy beneath my distant feet.

The officer spoke gruffly and then was silent again, listening.

He handed the cell back to me.

"You must go very quickly," Oméga told me. "I will stay on the phone until you are away. Do not insist. Leave now."

The officer motioned for the man holding Sola to release her. She walked toward me, glancing back, and I pointed at my camera. After a brief hesitation, during which he clenched his jaw, he extended it to me.

Sola and I hurried through the market to the main road and hailed a taxi. With my hand on the rusted edge of the open door, I paused, glancing back, still hoping for a glimpse of the white girl.

Beyond a row of shanties, a huddled cluster of small figures watched us. They evaporated into mirage-like shadow—dust blown into my eyes by a passing truck.

13

THE BALLAD OF THE BIG HOTEL

I was shaken by dreams: my father in a white undershirt, showing me the engorged veins in his arms, his skin blue in the wan light of a cold dawn—and then those same arms cradled a snowy, long-haired cat that would later escape into the yard and be torn apart by his dogs. Unable to express his sadness, he'd paced the house, trying to find where it had gotten free, so desperate to place the blame that he'd repeatedly asked me if I'd accidentally let it out.

Each time I woke, I sensed a misted figure just out of sight, in the room's pulsating dark. By morning, when I climbed out of bed, I was soaked with sweat and my legs felt rickety.

Sola hadn't stayed over, and I was glad not to have subjected her to my terrors, but as the taxi carried me to the airport, I regretted the night alone. I felt as if I'd lost my ballast, unable to move in straight lines, each memory of her or each glimpse of the cataclysmic city like an ocean swell unfurling inside my head. As I knew from past experiences, tears would come months or even years later.

I would hear or smell something that would remind me of what had happened at the market, or I would simply make a rarely used gesture, and my brain would release the long-contained emotions. Then I'd cry for a few minutes, and it would be over.

After takeoff, the drab, heavily settled outskirts of Kinshasa gave way to forest marked by the red, earthen sherds of settlements. The landscape was partitioned here and there by lines where forest and savannah met, and above all by the bulging, splintering river that descended from the north and which, were I attentive, I would see again in a few hours, on the other side of its immense curve.

I rested my forehead against the window, letting the vibrations of the engines calm me. Clouds boiled out of the forests, gathering against some high, cold limit of the atmosphere. The forests themselves bulged, parturient, ready to offer up the craving of the time: people for the slave trade; rubber and ivory during the colonial period; industrial grade diamonds to cut the steel of precision engines for jet fighters and tanks at the height of the Cold War; and more recently, coltan.

A few hours later, we glided over the hills of North Kivu, where the eastern horizon was a volcanic bulwark separating the Congo from Rwanda, and I stared down past the great axillary feather of the plane as it banked and landed.

I went through the usual security hassles and monetary requests, but Oméga had given me a sheaf of formal papers, and each time the agents hesitated over one, asking whether I had permission from all relevant authorities to be traveling in this region as a journalist, I offered another, until, resigned, they finally let me pass.

Oméga had told me that Baraka, a friend of his, would meet me in Goma and that he himself would be there a few days later for a conservation conference in a hotel, where the subject of Terra's disappearance would be addressed. He said that I should be certain to attend so he could facilitate introductions.

Baraka was waiting in the baggage claim. He was tall, with such poise that his thinness suggested elegance rather than hunger. His glasses had polished wire rims, and he wore his ironed police uniform with the neatness of a suit.

"Oméga told me you are a writer not only of journalism but of novels," he said as we crossed the hot, sunlit tarmac of the parking lot.

"I've written a few," I admitted, a detail I generally kept to myself since it often suggested to others a level of success that I didn't feel.

"I'm a poet," he replied. "That's the bond I share with Oméga. He has the soul of a poet. You have heard him preach?"

"Actually, I haven't."

"Ah. I was under the impression that you were close friends. He has certainly followed your work."

We'd reached his motorcycle, but he hesitated, his fingers resting on the dented metal of the gas tank.

"Before I drive you to the hotel," he said, "would you permit me to read you a poem?"

"Of course. I would love that," I told him, trying to sound enthusiastic.

He slipped a square of paper from his breast pocket, unfolded it, and held it before his face. The lines where it had been pleated were so worn through that I could see one of his eyes. Isolated from his face, it revealed a quality of stillness I'd observed only in the gazes of those in love.

Ode to UNICEF

the tables are single planks with tin bowls
the watery soup is the color of lead
a mineral we do not speak of here
where our gold is the color of bread
but children with the eyes of owls
wing the counting shadow to nourish fear

O UNICEF!—we read your posters and signs
and learn that far away rich men buy us
what is left after the sale of what is best
though their national lips drink from our mines
that make children who will never kiss
the perfume of a mother's breast

O' Congo, hungry on the scraps of UNICEF
O' UNICEF, fat on the grease of the Congo!

Ceremoniously, he refolded the paper and returned it to his shirt pocket.

"What do you think?" he asked.

"It's great," I said.

"Truly?"

"Yes, though I'm not sure the last two lines are necessary."

His lips compressed into a thin seam, and his expression became frosty.

"I'm no schoolboy and wasn't asking for corrections."

He got on his motorcycle, motioned for me to mount

behind him, and then drove me through Goma, over crumbled asphalt and along dusty straightaways, slowing where volcanic rock protruded from the dirt.

The city had thrived since my last visit. Shops and roadside vendors had multiplied, and men pushed bundles of clothes or bags of produce on handcarts whose every piece—even the wheels—was carved from wood. More vehicles plied the streets, though most bore the logos of humanitarian organizations.

"I'm not angry," Baraka said when we reached my hotel. "You're a technical sort of writer, a journalist and a composer of books for popular consumption." He touched his chest. "But poetry comes from the genius in our hearts. To change it would be to insult the spirit that brings it, and its inspiration is always justified by history. I have other poems. Poems of sadness for small NGOs that vanish before they start, or those that paint their acronyms on walls and yet seem not to exist but for the plump white people who eat in restaurants at night with prostitutes."

He lowered his jaw, taking a moment to swallow.

"I will return in the morning," he said more quietly. "The drive to where Terra worked is long, but we can do it in a day if we start early."

"I won't be keeping you from your job as an officer, will I?"

He lifted a hand above our heads, in a classical, faintly Italianate fashion, as if he might again recite verse.

"My work," he said, "is the idea of work. I am but the idea of an officer. Tomorrow, I will not be wearing this uniform, so I will be a motorcycle driver for a *mzungu*. Someday, I will cease to put this uniform on and will never drive anyone unless it be for love and friendship."

He punctuated his last word with a nod and departed

on his motorcycle, which tomorrow would take us over the road on which Terra had vanished, to the communities she'd tried to serve, where Richmond Hew was now in the process of establishing—through intermediaries in the Congolese government—a vast park.

I checked in at the hotel reception and climbed three flights of stairs to my room. Its window overlooked the great cauldron of Lake Kivu whose horizon fused with the sky, separating only when the sun drifted to the west and infused the air and water with a spectrum of earthen yellows and bruised, windy reds.

After changing, I continued watching the sunset on the restaurant terrace. I had seafood stew, followed by grilled tilapia garnished with fresh herbs and lime. The foreign staff of development organizations smoked, drank, and chattered as the lake's surface mirrored tendrils of clouds unwinding from volcanoes.

I again thought of my childhood novels: setting out, seeking purpose to measure one's agency, journeying to oppose evil, to confront what of that face one sees in the mirror. There is a woman to be won over, and an ally whose motivations can hardly be known but whose presence is crucial for success—whose existence is a lesson in trusting the unknown. But discovery no longer seemed so innocent, for me or for the Disney-eyed expats admiring the twilight.

I was feeling shaky again. I paid, tipped, and tottered back to my room.

I didn't want to sleep. I feared that the Pentus was exerting an adverse power over my brain, hijacking its pathways, recoding its signals. Its effect was supposed to weaken between the weekly doses, so maybe my mental disquiet was the result of stress—of so many articles to write if I wanted to make this trip lucrative.

Before going to sleep, I called Sola, and she answered, herself in bed at her hotel. We spoke softly, sharing details of our days. Being in foreign countries made such quick intimacy possible, which often led to expats rapidly shacking up. She told me that she'd had her driver call the pimps again, but with no luck. Now she was listening to the audio recordings of Bram's conversations with the girl.

"What are they like?"

"Sad. He's interested in sorcery but hardly at all in her life. The phenomena to which he applies his theories—her nonlinearity or duality or atemporality—seem to be the result of her making up the story on the go, in response to his questions."

I nearly asked if she was going to transcribe the conversation properly but caught myself, and just listened until she had worn out the subject of Rees.

After saying good night, I meditated. Years before, during a period when I'd done this often, I'd talked less, listened more, and didn't chase every mental association with a sense of the imminent discovery of a frontier to my self.

Meditating now, I realized that I was afraid to sleep, to return to my dreams. Then there was a brief spell of stillness: an awareness of the electrical tension between my skin and the air, of the unceasing flicker of uncoalesced thoughts in my brain, and of muted, incomplete impulses to action at the base of my skull and along my spine. From that space, recollections arose from the time when I'd published a memoir about my youth, my father's criminality, and the way a son grows into his father's shadow—though I hadn't been able to bring myself to write everything.

That night, despite a few impressions of the misted river, I slept well and woke knowing that the omitted memories were linked to my dreams. The sun was clambering up the other side of Rwanda's volcanoes. I dressed and met Baraka outside the gates.

"There is something I must do before I leave," he said, "something I do every morning in Goma."

His motorcycle was loaded with supplies for our trip, food and water bottles strapped behind the seat with thin strips of rubber cut from the blown tubes of tires.

I squeezed on behind him, the space so limited that my pelvis pressed to his buttocks. He drove us to another hotel, also on the lakeshore, but this one larger and uglier, older—an unlit bastion against the livid plain of the lake.

He shut off the engine, and we dismounted and stood in the blue shadow, with a ledge of dawn high above us, over the mountains to the east.

One by one, young women began leaving the hotel—dozens of them, beautiful and neatly dressed, following the same rusty path worn into the roadside weeds.

Baraka took a piece of paper from his pocket and read from it, speaking to the hotel.

your cells are the rooms of my brain
each night she lies down in all of them
the way pain inhabits imagination's prism
the way broken light undresses into color
I do not blame her for what I could not offer
I do not hate my earth for these dusty palms

He fell silent, staring first at the hotel and then at the brightening sky, his eyes so wide that he seemed to be rinsing them in the ambient glow.

"I've been trying to finish this poem for months," he said. "I'm writing it to the hotel that has taken her, but inspiration must pass through the heart, and there's too much pain in mine for the words to enter."

"She works there?" I asked.

He gestured loosely to the building's bulky silhouette. The bolt on the metal gate slid and clanged faintly, and the hinges creaked as another young woman slipped out.

"They all work there in a sense. They work, hoping for work to become love, if not with one man, then with the next one stationed here."

The dawn was now silvery and electric, and the blaze of sunrise lowered from the mountains like an immense, luminous drawbridge.

"I have loved her since she was a girl," Baraka told me.

The land around me felt more alive. I couldn't stop looking. Pale rocks along the shore. Long, soft water. Slender, pliable sprouts of weeds and wild grass. All of them seemed to be revealing themselves.

Baraka touched my shoulder. "We should go."

He climbed onto the motorcycle, and I joined him, again struggling to squeeze between him and the bundle of goods. We were disconcertingly close. He began to accelerate, but then slowed.

Over his shoulder, he asked, "You are married?"

"Yes," I lied. "I am."

He nodded, as if reassured that, at least for today, he was safe from the rapacity of white lust.

14

THE IMPORTANCE OF GENRES

&

THE STORM

The motorcycle carried us out of the city, between orchards and fields planted along steep slopes. Big trucks loaded with produce passed in the other direction, their tops crowded with workers whose legs hung from the sides, the soles of their bare feet intimate and vulnerable just above our heads.

The truck tires lifted so much dust that Baraka slowed and kept to the shoulder, and I narrowed my eyes, grit in my lashes. Cumulonimbi towered over us with the energy of living creatures claiming the sky. We rode eagerly into their mothering shadows, where even the dust felt less aggressive.

Among our many conversations that day, Baraka told me that he'd named himself for Obama. He'd had a previous name, one without destiny, he said, showing me the back of his hand in a dismissive gesture.

During one of our breaks to drink water and eat pale clods of fermented manioc—ever so faintly cheesy, with a texture of hard, half-dried putty—I proposed writing an article about him and his poetry.

"I think it could be interesting to a Western audience. You and your poetry really capture what's happening here—the dominance of the NGOs alongside the exploitation of foreign powers. I would show your writing as a cultural expression of the Congo's chaos after the wars . . ."

With a sudden motion, as if stung, he reached quickly for his glasses, took them off and removed a scrap of red fabric from inside his jacket. He snapped it in the air, rubbed it over the lenses, returned it to his inner pocket, and the glasses to his face. I now saw how stern and evaluating his look had become.

"I do not wish," he said, "to be a sad, comic figure for one of those evaporating internet articles that always appears to be new but is always the same."

The manioc I'd just bitten clotted in my mouth, and though I had an urge to spit it out, or choke, I abided its liquefaction.

"I don't see you that way," I finally said.

"You do not?" he asked, his eyes so still and hard that I found it difficult to believe I'd seen them look on his verse with so much love. "You truly do not?"

He kept staring, as if the power of his gaze would refute mine.

"I don't," I repeated, now less certain. The article would have been easy to flip, and perhaps it would have contained some sad and comic elements, as were customary in the genre.

He appeared to read something in my face, gave an abbreviated nod, and turned back to the food.

"Now is not the time to write about me," he said over his shoulder. "I do not care to be a fraught glimpse of my people's humanity, engrossed with the sort of futile romanticism with which your people, being so self-assured, can't be bothered. Besides, an artist must know when to reveal himself to the world. It's too soon."

He broke off a piece of manioc and chewed, facing the green, conical mountains rising above the farmed ridgelines to the east.

Soon, we were on the motorcycle again, and I was wondering whether, in the eyes of friends back home, I appeared absurd, less driven by convictions than tilting after them.

A dozen hours passed before the road narrowed. It split repeatedly, snaking up between forested summits. The air was damp, suddenly cool as our lengthening shadows pointed the way. Sunset mantled the mountainous horizon at our backs.

In small valleys, there were villages or scattered homes, and then the road became muddy, flanked by elephant grass so high I had the impression of riding inside a tunnel of thatch.

The exposed red earth narrowed to a trail that ended at a small white house perched on a mountainside of dense forest. The concrete slab before it had steps leading down to a second platform cluttered with crates and plastic barrels. Further steps descended to a third platform, on which sat a smaller house. Its windows were lit, and smoke rose from a metal pipe.

The first house, I learned, belonged to Terra, and in her absence, I would sleep there. The lower one was where Sébastien, her cook, lived. He plodded up the steps to greet us, stooped and with an air of frailty that could have been elderliness or disposition. His short cropped hair was black, and his gauntness might have resulted from hunger, illness, age, a life of exertion, or all four. His large, faintly hooded eyes evoked a wary, patient resignation. He might have been fifty or seventy-five.

"I will make you dinner," he told me, "but it will take a while. Please rest."

He then explained to Baraka where he could find a place to stay in the nearby village. I paid Baraka, gave him money for food and lodging, and wished him good night.

Terra's house was a single room. A narrow back door led to an open-air shower enclosed by tall, woven fibers. After undressing, I stood beneath the spigot, shivering as cold water fell on my head. I rinsed the dust from my hair, eyes, and skin, and then turned the knob and hurried back inside.

I dressed and descended the stairs and knocked. Sébastien opened the door and motioned to the table where he'd set out a plate and silverware. The room was otherwise empty, its concrete walls painted white. A door led to the kitchen, and he passed through it to check the pots on the fires before returning to the table.

"Do you have any news of Madame Terra?" he asked.

"No. Nothing. You?"

"Nothing. Local chiefs have spoken with the Hutu rebel leaders who still live in the mountains, and they have no information. Normally, they keep to themselves. This is not a good time to draw attention, and they are rebels only in name. They have been living in the forests for twenty years. A generation has grown up since the genocide in Rwanda or their parents' decision to come here. They are traders now and hunters, and Terra worked well with them. I do not believe they would harm her."

"Then who would?" I asked, not wanting to mention Hew. He must have been nearby—in a village or the forests, laying the groundwork to establish a park—and he almost certainly would have heard about my arrival.

Sébastien stood with his arms slack, the posture suggesting reluctance to use more energy than absolutely necessary. He blinked thoughtfully, the skin of his eyelids so thin I had the impression he could see through them.

"We do not know," he said. "It would be hard to keep a secret here. Maybe the other rebels, the M23. They are like the Tutsis in Rwanda and work with them to smuggle coltan and diamonds, though they say they have been mistreated since the end of the war and not given the positions of power the government promised. But if they kidnapped her, they would sell her back. If they killed her, they would brag."

He returned to the kitchen to stir his pots and when he neared the table again, I refrained from asking about Hew. It was too soon. The danger with journalism was that if you arrived with a sense of the truth, people often confirmed it so as to be helpful.

Sébastien served me dinner—chopped forest mushrooms and a plate of greens cooked in palm oil, and rice in which grit crunched between my teeth. He told me that the next day, if I wanted, he could buy meat.

I ate quickly, and when I'd finished, he pulled out a chair and asked if I'd brought any books in French.

I'd been traveling with two battered classics, the first Martiniquan and the second Acadian: *Texaco,* by Patrick Chamoiseau, and *Pélagie-la-Charette,* by Antonine Maillet. His posture shifted, as if he were waking up, and he asked if he could read one that night, and I said of course.

"I love every kind of book," he told me, "but new books are hard to come by, and the more a book is from far away, the more I love it, because that is what a book is for—to show you far-off places, so you can see and touch all that would normally be hidden. Sometimes, I read a very real, very hard and real book, and it makes me sad for the life I have lived and the old man I am becoming. I feel the pain of time in my bones. As you get older, there is less padding between the world and your bones, so lying to yourself about the truths of existence becomes more difficult. But sometimes I read books with magic, in other lands, and I think that if I had left home younger, I could have found a better life, because that is what the heroes are always doing. There are enemies and monsters to be fought, but at the end of that, there is always a better life. And I also read horror books because the world is full of terrors, of things that eat you, of people who look at you with eyes like fangs, and after each story of horror, I am grateful. I have lived the horror in my mind and survived it, and I am stronger, more alive. And I even love those books you whites so enjoy, about how to improve every aspect of yourself, how to cure your wife's unhappiness by thanking her and making her feel special for the chores women have done since the dawn of time, and how to look in the mirror and admire the man staring back at you as if Jesus were just behind the glass, whispering that you are perfect. When I read them, I see myself as a wealthy general with a dozen happy wives and a hundred adoring children, and I picture a national disaster and everyone asking me for the solution, and I realize that I would be as good if not better than any other man to lead my people. Even after I wake from this dream, I don't feel deceived, and for days afterward, I walk a little lighter. But in truth, I prefer books of the technological future in which we can repair anything, even our bodies and our minds, or go to other planets, and I am sad because I was born too early and because these stories—which will someday happen without me—they tell me the truth of how soon my life will be forgotten. I am sad because my world"—here he motioned with a scraggy hand to indicate all that existed beyond the small room—"did not become everything that I can imagine."

I felt tenderness tinged with a condescending sympathy that I tried to erase. And briefly, I wished I'd never been corrupted by academia and could enjoy any story I encountered, as I had when I was a child, reading whatever I could find, not discerning between sci-fi, fantasy, the classics, or my mother's books on the many paths to self-transformation and harmony with existence.

I told him that on my computer I had numerous novels in French, in digital form—dozens at least—and that if we could find a printer, he could read them.

He nodded, stood, and left the room while I sat with my thoughts, hating the presumption of superiority within my sentiments—that reading was somehow more for me, even as I feared it might somehow be less, that I might read while experiencing limited change, affirming what I knew rather than expanding.

Sébastien returned with a black fanny pack, sat down and unzipped it. He took out a small, bone-handled knife with a hide sheath, set it on the table, and then a roll of francs in small denominations. He began counting.

"I should have enough to print a few."

"But I must pay you for your work," I told him, "and for letting me stay here."

"The house is Madame Terra's. You came to help, so the only cost is food."

"I insist on paying for your work. It's only fair."

He slipped the bills and knife back into the fanny pack.

He nodded, though accepting my offer seemed to cause him pain.

"You are the one doing me the favor," I said. "Thank you for dinner."

But even as I climbed the two flights of steps to Terra's house, I disliked my feeling of power. I'd done nothing to deserve it, and yet, oddly, that I could admit this to myself made me feel unpleasantly righteous.

A storm woke me that night. There was an intense dark, so thick and stifling that I gasped just to prove to myself that I could breathe. Lightning outlined the structure of the house, its fulmination infusing every gap in the wood, every joint, so that, when the darkness reasserted itself, the skeleton of the house—compact and thoracic—smoldered in my retinas, with me inside it.

Thunder followed, the room shaking and the chatter of nocturnal insects quieting. Lightning flashed again and again, and the booms came faster, chasing the light, the storm galloping toward me. Wind howled. Rain scoured the walls. The house glowed, and I lay as if in the ribs of a whale, trying to cohere a few thoughts of peace—the sorts of notions I'd like to have before departing this world: love and forgiveness, remembrance of kindness, beauty and connection, calmness in the face of letting go. But the storm's immediacy held me in thrall, and the glimmer of beatitude was dim, far away in my mind—like a penny at the bottom of a well.

And then silence. My bare feet on the cold concrete slab of the floor was an unexpected joy, an encounter with a loved one in a place far from home. I unlatched the door and opened it. There was nothing. No moon. No stars. Panic began to fill me, to blur out my reconnection with life. The storm had come during a dream, and the dream hadn't quite ended, and I now had a strong sense that Baraka's words had been accurate—that I didn't write from my heart. I offered no practical solutions, no visions of the future. I was a cipher, a dragoman, a paraphrast for the lives of others. I felt like a cheap plastic pen lying in the gravel of a parking lot. Something had been on the verge of revealing itself but then had deemed me unworthy and moved on.

I lit a candle. Humidity glittered in the air. Outside, the mist was so thick that I couldn't see the platform. I realized what had happened. My nightmares of the past that I hadn't written had rushed back with renewed violence, trying to get into the house, and the storm had been their fury.

I waited for the mist to intrude upon the room, to claim the air and fill my lungs and eyes, but it just turned in a slow eddy around the house, a few tendrils caressing the doorframe like fingers.

I did sleep again, but fitfully, as the lightning-infused house, the moonlit river, and my father—images of him fractured across his life—all strobed inside my brain.

In the morning, I assembled my francophone e-books on a zip drive. Most were Québécois authors, some African, others French—many of them friends.

When Baraka stopped by to see how I was doing, I gave him the drive and money for printing costs. He rode the two hours into town and returned that evening with a bundle of paper a foot thick wrapped with strips of inner tubes and tied awkwardly behind the seat.

I was just coming back from interviewing men who'd worked with Terra in the forests, who'd tracked the gorillas with her and helped with animal censuses and biodiversity studies—all of whom said that they either didn't know Hew or hadn't seen him in over a decade.

The sun had set, and the path along the ridge offered a vista on the hundreds of domed peaks that ran on to the southwest—the product of millennia of rain on the soft, eroded earth that had been uplifted in the volcanic convulsions around the Great Rift Valley. In the misted dusk, the summits coalesced into an impression of incoming waves.

Near the house, Sébastien was waiting on the road—perhaps having heard the sound of Baraka's motorcycle echoing in the mountains or simply having become anxious with nightfall, waiting for me to return. Or perhaps he'd been thinking of Terra.

His eyes were narrowed, their corners drawn down, and his expression was that of enduring a familiar pain. I wanted to believe I knew that pain, but I probably didn't.

15

AN ORAL TALE: DEATH OF A CONSERVATIONIST

That night, after a dinner of chicken boiled with red chili pepper, its juice poured over the gritty rice and greens, Sébastien sat across from me at the table.

"And have you found useful information in your interviews?"

"Yes. The people speak very highly of Terra."

He nodded faintly, slowly, lowering his eyes. The monk-like stillness of his face alerted me. I'd seen similar expressions in the past, during interviews, usually before all I believed to be true inverted itself.

I took a slow breath. The hikes all day, between ranger stations and villages, on steep paths, in the etheric mountain air, had been invigorating, but now the muscles around my ribs felt tired.

As if on cue, Sébastien asked, "What makes you believe the people you interview are telling you the truth?"

"Why wouldn't they?"

"What reason do they have to trust you? If a stranger

came asking questions, and you had to make a wager, how would you do it?"

A translucent green moth had slipped into the room and, as I considered his question, it circled the naked bulb hanging from the ceiling.

"It would depend on what was at stake."

"Exactly," he said, his face still the one that people wore when deciding whether to reveal a new perspective.

"You're saying that they might ask themselves what they had to gain from telling the truth or what they had to lose."

"Yes," he said, "but they might also ask how many truths they should give. Knowledge is an intuitive barter. Should they give it all and be left empty-handed?"

"But what would they have to gain from holding it back?"

"The question is what would they have to lose by giving all of it."

He sat, watching me—his smile so imperceptible it seemed less a change in his expression than an illusion cast by the occasional weakening of the electric current that dimmed the bulb.

"So," I said, "they know I believe Terra was good, and they are confirming that. And maybe she was good in some ways, and what they say is true. There is no danger in confirming my belief in her goodness, whether she comes back or is gone forever. But maybe she was also bad in some ways, and telling me this could be a risk for them if she returns. And if she stays vanished and the investigation into her death continues, the bad things they say about her could turn them into suspects."

The green moth collided with the bulb and fell, twitching on the table. Sébastien pinched one of its diaphanous wings and tossed the creature, very deliberately, into the corner of the room. It fell right below a fissure in the wood, and a gray wolfish spider the size of a child's hand darted out, gripped the squirming creature in its mandibles, and withdrew.

"Are you ready to interview me?" he asked.

"Is this a good time?"

"It is."

I took my recorder out of my camera bag and set it on the table.

"My story," he said, his eyes lowered, "begins in 1947. It was thirteen years before Independence, the year that my mother was floated in Lake Kivu to die. This was a punishment, a way of disposing of women for their failures. Her failure among her people in Rwanda is not mine to speak of, even if I am the fruit of that failure. In the lake, she was saved by a Congolese fisherman, and though she soon became his second wife and had to learn a new language, she was able to speak the words of her childhood to a few other mothers in the village who had themselves been set adrift as girls, well before her.

"Growing up as an outsider teaches one the visceral meaning of injustice. This is how I came to fight for Laurent-Désiré Kabila during the years of the revolution, when I was only thirteen. You may not believe what I will say next. That is your choice. I met Che Guevara. I carried a bag for him through the forest. For such a great man, he had fragile lungs. Following behind him, I could see his strength filling him the way a man's shadow, in the moment before the sun reaches the horizon, reveals his determination. But his body struggled to follow. It made me admire him so much more, though years later I regretted reading his harsh sentences about the Congolese, our lack of discipline in the struggle against imperialism, and I felt that he might have let his frustration get the better of him. Removing the grip of colonialism—both within and without—has never been easy.

"I would like to say that he left me with kind or wise words that have since become a lesson for me. He didn't. The only lesson he imparted was determination, absolute certainty. You might ask why I am not a general, or a president, or a rich man. My triumph is the beating of my heart, and my education. I was thirteen when I first took up arms. I fought my way into manhood. I saw the men around me become something terrible, and I promised myself that I would not. I would strive for Che's dignity."

Sébastien sat differently now, it seemed to me, though I acknowledged to myself that I might be seeing him through the filter of his story. Rather than a thin, aging cook, he appeared distinguished—a commander marshaling the characters of his past. I noticed then a small, tarnished metal pin on the green cloth of his lapel, and though I could not make out the symbol imprinted on it, I imagined that it represented a military cause from long ago.

"There were of course empty years," he said. "Mobutu took over the country, and the United States and Europe gave him the money to become the world's greatest dictator. He plundered the Congo and let it fall to pieces so that its people became strangers to each other. We couldn't unify to resist him. Travel and communication became exhausting. Survival was divisive.

"My empty years ended one day, here in the forest, where I'd decided to hunt for bush meat and sell it to survive. I was looking for whatever I could find, and I came upon men who'd killed a family of gorillas. I remember the large black bodies glistening with blood, the layers and layers of muscle when the skin was peeled back. But what I remember most clearly are the baby gorillas, tied up on the ground, crying. They were crying. I asked the men why they had not killed them, and they said they would sell them as pets or eat them fresh later. They already had enough meat that was going to spoil if they didn't work fast.

"That night, lying in my camp beneath a tree, I couldn't stop thinking about the crying gorillas. I didn't dare speak of them. They weren't human, and there was so much human suffering that I asked myself how I could care that animals suffered. But then I understood that they weren't merely animals but children crying. Maybe they did not have our words or our ways. But their pain was a language I knew.

"A few years later, I heard that the Virunga National Park was hiring guards. It is, as you must know, Africa's first national park, and I considered how profound it would feel to take care of it and its animals and above all its mountain gorillas. But being a guard there was not what many imagine. We were trained like soldiers. We had shootouts with poachers. This bothered me, since I wanted to protect the park for our people, not from those of us who were starving and had to hunt to survive. But I continued, until I met Richmond Hew."

If the story of his past had transformed Sébastien, then this disclosure turned him into a master of chiaroscuro. The electric current did in fact dim with the leeching of electricity from the line or a flagging at the source—a small microhydro generator installed in a mountain creek I'd seen earlier that day.

"So you know Richmond Hew?"

"I do. I worked for him for years. Did you think Terra was the one who built these houses, who poured all this concrete?"

"I assumed so . . ."

"She did not. Hew was here first, during the war. He did not leave once. There were no vacations for the comforts of home. There were no little medical questions that he wanted to have checked out in a proper hospital."

Sébastien spoke as if quoting, and I feared that he might admire Hew.

"Hew was a hard employer," he said, "but he never struck me, because he knew my story. He had asked, and I had told it. He struck others when it was merited. Seeing a white hand hit flesh awakens an old trauma in us, so I hated him at times. I still hate him. But I am jumping ahead. We will get to the part when you ask me about the horrible things he did, and I will tell you one or two, but for now, let me share what was good.

"Hew had heard about my efforts in Virunga and hired me to help him. That was thirty years ago. He lived out here like a man for whom there was nothing else. I do not know his story. I don't know where he came from or what he missed. He wouldn't speak of it. He never drank. He awoke first each dawn and was already outside, in the forest, taking notes. There was a silence around him. I thought about that silence, and I came to believe that it was the silence of a man for whom himself, his body, is secondary to his goal—much as was the case for Che.

"But I saw a change in him during those years. Conservation organizations were throwing money at the mountain gorillas while he was trying to prevent the next great wildlife slaughter. He said that the bean counters had taken over the world, and not until the supply of eastern lowland gorillas was critically depleted would their value rise.

"Then the war came. He negotiated with rebels to continue his work, even as they stole his supplies. He never complained, though he sometimes took violent action if someone was hunting gorillas.

"His change occurred at the height of the war, when the butchery of the wildlife could no longer be prevented. Masses of hungry soldiers—both Congolese and foreign—slaughtered every ape, okapi, and elephant they could find. Lakes with thousands of hippopotami were suddenly empty. That's when Hew became ruthless. He realized that he needed money and had to position himself where the attention of the world would fall. You might be asking yourself if he cared about nature. He did. He cared about it in the way that only a man who hates society truly can.

"When he left to protect okapis, he had not given up here. He brought Terra to us. She never tells that part of the story. She didn't want a park, since then the government would have power and she would no longer control the funding. Was her model entirely bad? I hardly think so. But it was built around her. She didn't lift her hand in violence as often as Hew, but to say that her hand was eternally gentle would be a lie. She confronted her enemies as we all do, and she rallied her allies. The communities protected the gorillas and the forests under Terra as they had under Hew, but their generosity and labors became a sign of her power.

"When Hew returned, it was because the ongoing wars in the east had finally killed enough eastern lowland gorillas to make the faraway rich people care. I saw him only briefly.

We were like two old forest buffalos snorting in recognition of a distant past. That's how it was. Terra rushed to America to tell everyone that the harmonious communities she had created here would be destroyed. She leveled accusations against Hew about little girls and asked Parks International to send an independent investigator—a man who did come. That struck a terrible blow against Hew. Immediately, much of the donor money he had been receiving for his personal projects was sent elsewhere, but the big organizations still knew that he, more than anyone else, could mobilize the Congolese government to make parkland quickly."

"Do you know the name of the investigator?"

"Bradley," Sébastien said. "Bradley Moore."

"How long ago was he here?"

"About two months."

"And do you have any idea where he is now?"

"Somewhere in the center of the country, in Maniema Province, still looking for proof of Hew's misdeeds. I don't know what has happened to him."

Sébastien sat, his spine straight against the chair's backrest, his eyes half-lidded and his palms turned up in his lap, as if he were in a meditative trance. I regretted having interrupted the flow of his story and was thinking of what to ask next when he spoke.

"Though Hew's park won't be perfect," he said, "it will be good for us. There was always a threat that the merchants in Bukavu would convince landowners to cancel the agreements Terra had set up. That pressure increased with the rise in the price of lumber, which has been significant recently. The park we are making is a small one by all standards, occupying only the area where people do not cultivate, but it will create jobs on its outskirts. Will landowners lose some territory? Yes. But lose it or sell it, little will change in the end."

"Are there locals who support Terra's vision and who are willing to fight?"

He lifted his eyebrows slightly before he smiled.

"The park has already been made, and Hew has gone home."

"How did it happen so quickly?" I asked, sounding breathless and young to my own ears. I'd spent a day interviewing people here without anyone having revealed this to me.

"Hew was clever. He sent a message to the directors of Western conservation organizations that a white baby gorilla had been born in the high forests where poachers were likely to infiltrate and where Terra's community projects offered little protection. I believe that, until then, only one albino gorilla had been known to humans, a fellow named Snowflake who died of old age in a Spanish zoo. News of the albino—Hew nicknamed her Bianca—immediately reached the wealthiest donors. They supplied the money and the political pressure on the Congo to protect this rarity, and the park was immediately established."

"Why haven't I heard of this?" I asked.

"The organizations didn't want to go public until they had photos of Bianca. A team of biologists will arrive next week with a professional photographer. Unfortunately, there will be no photos for the newspapers of the world."

"Why not?"

"Because Bianca doesn't exist. I would have heard of this gorilla myself, long before Hew. The creature is Hew's invention."

The air had cooled, and I was aware of new sounds in the frantic nocturnal chirruping, behind the fiddling of insects and orgiastic ribbiting of frogs—a very faint, crystalline fluting, a night bird or the distilled strains of distant human activity.

A small window with a yellowed lace curtain framed the dark, and the only hint of moonlight was a pale warp in the glass.

"But I cannot defend Hew," Sébastien told me. "His good does not overshadow the bad. He did have an appetite for girls. Years ago, I met someone who worked with him in another part of the country. The man confided in me that Hew had gotten a thirteen-year-old Pygmy girl pregnant and that, when she told him, he drowned her in a river. Hew did this because Pygmies are inferior in the eyes of most Congolese and having a child with one could have damaged his reputation and power. But this is a story I heard from a man who may have been his enemy. Land is wealth and power, and after you create a park, the wealth and power do not disappear. They simply change hands."

I hesitated. "But you do not seem bothered by Hew's actions?"

He stared at me with a level, accustomed gaze, the way a man who has worked in a misty landscape all his life will stare through the fog, already seeing the shapes that will materialize when it disperses.

"If I do not appear outraged," he said slowly, as if with great fatigue, "it is because I have worked not only with many men, but with many whites."

Something in his eyes—a quality of self-possession or simply the settling weight of consciousness—became apparent, as if he were demonstrating how, with discipline, seeing could be a bodily experience for the one who is seen. I felt as if, seconds before, I'd been in many places at once, and now the versions of myself were slotted together, like cards into a deck. I was suddenly aware of the force of gravity and the material truth of my weight. The legs of my wooden chair ground faintly against the floor. Its crossbars creaked.

I stood and thanked him and said good night.

Returning to Terra's house, I paused to shake off the foreign feeling. When I opened the door, I did so slowly now that I knew Hew had once lived here.

16

A DOLE OF DOVES

Before dawn, I woke to a faraway engine. A motorcycle. It stopped, still at a distance. The air in the room was cold and damp as I lay beneath the blankets, tempted to relax back into sleep, but also listening. A sound outside. Maybe a footstep—the crunch of grit against concrete.

I eased myself out of bed and crouched by the window, pinched the corner of the curtain, and looked out. A pair of wet boot tracks led down the concrete steps. I could hear nothing. I was almost ready to give up when Baraka climbed the stairs very quietly, leaving Sébastien's house, and continued along the path. Five minutes later, the motorcycle started again. Then there was a swishing sound from the platform below. Sébastien was sweeping the steps.

I returned to the bed. The mattress had mostly cooled, but as I drew the sheet to my chin, I managed to find the faint core of warmth I'd left.

Two hours later, I still hadn't slept, and I went down and ate the eggs and rice that Sébastien had set out. We spoke of books as if our conversation the previous evening hadn't taken place. I offered the copies of *Texaco* and *Pélagie-la-Charette* as gifts to say thanks, since I'd read both. I rarely carried new books when traveling but rather those I wanted to reread and see in a different light. He again looked humbled and fragile as he nodded and thanked me, but mid-sentence he stiffened with an expression of listening.

"What is it?" I asked.

He held up a finger for silence.

There were the faint echoes of a distant sound, similar to that of someone chopping wood, which had been common enough during my walks through the mountains. But now the forests and villages were oddly hushed, even the birds quiet.

"Those were gunshots," he told me.

"Are you sure?" I said, but he cut me off with a glance. I'd heard weapons firing in Afghanistan and Iraq, both far and close, but the reports a moment ago had been muted, echoing beyond the ridgeline that sheltered the house.

Together, we climbed the steps until we reached the trail and could see down to where three men were running toward us.

"Do they have weapons?" I asked, squinting but unable to make out what they held.

"They're from the village. Something has happened."

Soon, I discerned their machetes, but these were commonly carried for work in the area.

Still running, the foremost began shouting to Sébastien in the local language.

Sébastien's right hand shook as he raised it in what appeared a reflexive gesture of shock.

"What?"

"Baraka," he said.

"What about him?"

"He's been shot."

Sébastien turned and looked into my eyes so directly, so openly, that I realized how rarely this happened between men.

"Is there a clinic nearby where we can take him?" I asked.

Sébastien was just staring at me, his eyes slightly jaundiced.

"He is dead."

I was aware of the early morning air on my skin and a feeling of time lapsing, of the first cold day of autumn back home, as my emotions conflated with memories I couldn't identify—scars of old pains that, like faint imperfections sensed beneath the fingertips, marked the surface of my mind.

Sébastien shouted something to the men, and they turned and raced back in the direction from which they'd come.

"Quick," he said. "Get your belongings."

I ran inside for my backpack and camera bag, and soon we were hurrying down the trail.

"Who did it?"

"I don't know. They took his motorcycle, so it was a theft. Since he is not from here, he was vulnerable. Attackers would face retaliation within the communities if they harmed a local. I suspect they were sending a message."

"To me?"

"Yes."

"Why not just kill me?"

Coming up the trail toward us was a man on a motorcycle, its tires slipping a little on the damp earth.

"That would cause too much trouble."

The motorcycle stopped before us, and the driver turned it around. He was an older man with a drawn, pockmarked face and a long jaw.

"You must go," Sébastien told me.

"What about Baraka?"

"There's nothing for you to do. It's best you leave immediately."

As I climbed onto the back of the seat, I thought about Baraka's sneak visit that morning. Maybe all this was a ploy and he wasn't really dead. But I couldn't imagine it serving any purpose, since I was already leaving.

The driver released the brakes, and as we began to roll, I twisted in my seat to say goodbye to Sébastien. I could read no betrayal in him, only sadness and outrage.

He lifted a hand and I did too, and then I faced ahead so as not to unbalance my driver. He was a smaller man, shakier in his navigation of the ruts and mud slicks. The motorcycle was red, and I feared it might be Baraka's, but I wasn't able to recall the details of the one we'd ridden in on, not even its color.

Ahead, where the trail narrowed through a stretch of dense forest, a few dozen people had gathered. They backed into each other, opening a passage, all staring at me, the women and men expressionless, simply looking hard at my face, not as if searching but as if taking me in, remembering.

At their center, a small wet patch darkened the earth of the roadway. Their gazes dropped as our tires cut through it, leaving a deep track.

In a stand of weeds, a body lay on a wooden cart. The arms and feet hung off, and a dirty green jacket had been draped over the face and chest. One hand was smeared with blood, congealed drops beading on each fingertip.

At some point farther down the mountain, the motorcycle fishtailed and the driver braked. I should have leaned with him. The earth slammed my chest, and my backpack went over my head, its straps cinching beneath my armpits. I curled onto my side as water soaked my pants. There were no sounds. I could take in only minute amounts of air. They gradually became a little deeper, until the muscles of my diaphragm relaxed.

The driver waited on the motorcycle, also muddied. He looked bored and impatient, as if I were obscuring the real tragedy. I found my camera bag and climbed back on behind him.

We didn't eat or even drink, and we didn't speak. Once on good roads, he drove faster than Baraka had.

Years ago, I'd read an online article on how to prevent conflict. It said that people reflect back to us what we perceive in them and that we should picture the child our rival had been, focus on the good and grow that. I'd done this in war zones, approaching foreign soldiers not as terrifying spectacles of male power but as sons, brothers or fathers. I'd felt how we can injure others with our fear, since it presumes their inhumanity.

The books scattered about my childhood home had primed me to see a world awaiting my gaze. They explained how to manifest dreams, forge a better self, strip away pain and regret, and live in purity. They meshed mysticism with fantasy and made me feel that I wasn't the child of an impoverished, broken family but an avatar of the universe, its billions of years leading up to me.

Maybe I had simply been seeing myself in every human

surface, negating the rage of others, protected not at all by my merit, though certainly protected.

The driver and I said nothing until Goma, when I told him the name of the hotel where I was supposed to meet Oméga for the conservation conference.

He pulled up to a large compound on the lakeside. I climbed off and he sped away without saying a word.

In the sudden, false silence after hours of the engine's metallic clattering, I felt nauseated. The hotel was the same one to which Baraka had read his poem. It was late afternoon, the sun an errant balloon drifting in mist over the western hills.

I knocked on the metal gate and the hotel guard let me inside.

After checking in, I took a long shower and wanted to sleep, but I dressed and walked down to the crowded conference hall. From across the room, Oméga saw me and hurried over.

"I'm glad that you're safe," he said. "I was afraid for you."

Behind him, a white man with a slight drawl of the American South was speaking on a wooden platform. Oméga observed my face as I tried to find words. He nodded, briefly closing his eyes, and then we both turned to listen. Gradually, I was able to release the tension in my throat.

The speaker was bald but for a ruff of red hair, as if he'd glued a tiny fox stole to the back of his head. A screen was next to him, and on it, a projector flashed a square of light and then an image of Terra.

He began talking about her achievements, about how much he admired her, how honored his organization had been to support her, but he kept calling her Terri. People in the audience repeatedly whispered, "Terra," until he stopped, agape.

"What? What's that? Terra? Oh. Oh my God. Of course. Terra."

He laughed, and his audience tittered in support.

"We're going to play a slideshow and some video that our team put together. It's an homage of sorts, not an in memoriam. Let's pray that we're a half century away from that. This will show her work, her connection, her sense of humor and just how, how . . ." He hesitated, his eyes bulging, since—we would all understand a second later—he'd just realized what he was about to say: "how alive she was."

Finishing, he turned quickly to face the screen.

Images and very short videos of her work followed: Terra coordinating in the forests with her trackers, Terra playing peekaboo with an orphaned gorilla, and then Terra in a boat with two white men and a few Congolese. The camera swung to the shore where a teenage boy, young and finely muscled and extremely handsome, was standing at the water's edge naked. He thrust out his pelvis as if to say "You looking at this?" and shook his cock at them.

The people on the boat broke into nervous laughter.

Man One (British accent): What's he trying to say?

Man Two (Canadian accent): Something about being enthusiastic and naked.

Man One: Maybe he's offering services.

Terra: I'd hire him.

Man Two: No, I think he was just feeling spontaneously inspired to share.

Man One: Maybe it's like mooning. Maybe he's telling us to fuck off.

Man Two: I think it can be all of the above.

Terra: He's a very pretty boy.

The audience laughed, and the speaker with the reddish ruff said, "Well, I don't know who put that homage together, but it looks as if the buffet has arrived."

The hotel staff was wheeling in three tables covered with platters of cheese, crudités, shrimp, and smoked salmon.

I glanced at Oméga, and he motioned to a tall, thin man with a dusty pallor who hovered at the buffet, encroaching, his eyes like those of a snake inspecting eggs in a nest.

"We will discuss Baraka later," Oméga said. "For now, we must ensure that you complete your investigation."

I nodded, relieved to be able to focus on anything else. I stepped toward the man and asked if I could speak with him.

Without turning from the buffet, he looked at me. His gray crew cut was streaked with white, and tiny, white, wormlike hairs protruded from his nostrils.

"I was wondering if I might ask you a few questions about Richmond Hew."

"Ah, Hew!" he said in an American accent, raising his voice as if to exalt him, but then lowered it. "Why are you asking?"

"I'm a journalist, and I've been investigating his projects."

"Well, I worked with him years ago in the north of the country. An impressive man. Impressive." He hesitated and raised his eyebrows, scanning the buffet, and repeated one last time, sounding more resigned, "Impressive."

Though he was now turned away from the food, one of his arms extended like a vulture's neck behind him and his hand lowered in the shape of a beak to nab a shrimp and bring it back to his mouth. He did it without looking, as if he'd survived decades of conferences because of adaptation to this form of sustenance.

"Okay, so Hew," he said, "you want to know some general things about him?"

"That would be a good place to start."

"Well, let's see. He's been working on okapis, a sort of short-necked forest giraffe—one of those bread-and-butter animals that can bring in troves of grants for conservationists. By the way, this is all off the record. At least for now. Let's talk, and later you can say what you want to use, and I'll tell you whether it's on the record."

"Sure," I replied, not expecting much more than vague leads.

"So yeah, where to go with this story?" he muttered. "Hew abandons the gorillas that were less lucrative—at least back then. There was Okapi Girl—an Irish woman, I guess, in the okapi range—but that's what we called her. Apparently, she had a pony fetish as a child and read about striped endangered forest ponies here. Something like that."

"Got it. Makes more sense than a giraffe fetish."

"To you, maybe. But she was already there when Hew went out. I don't know what happened to her. A story a bit like Terra's, but I believe she took her own life. A decade of isolation, failed dreams, and no funding. I don't really know. Hew was blamed. She'd been there for years, and he showed up and took it all over, though of course another version of the story has it that she changed her malaria medication and began hallucinating and running naked through the forests. She probably got bit by a snake."

My pulse stuttered as cold apprehension moved through me.

His beak-like hand, having nabbed its fourth shrimp, was bringing it back to his mouth.

"And what else?" he said. "Well, there's Terra. Jesus. Can

you imagine a twenty-four-year-old woman moving to the Congo and staying through the war? Hew has three decades under his belt. He doesn't even come back to America anymore. He has a chain of intermediaries. But the guy, he fucking delivers. Basically, an organization gets a huge grant and channels some of the money to him. He writes up a report based on what he's been working on for years. They receive it along with some photos of smiling Pygmies and they use that material to make their donors happy."

"We're getting into territory where I have questions I'd like to have on the record," I told him.

"I'm not surprised," he said as his arm extended again—elegantly reaching between two other people now feeding off the buffet—and caught another large pink shrimp. After chewing, he added, "But let's hold off. Best to talk this through and decide what should really be on the record."

"Have you heard of Bradley Moore?" I asked.

He squinted in thought—his expression as contrived as his discourse had sounded artificial.

"Yes, right. He's an independent investigator we hired to check out Hew."

"Have you received much back from him?"

"No. Very little."

"Has he disappeared?"

"I don't know. He's certainly been slow to give us updates."

"Why are you having Hew investigated?"

"We like to keep him on a shorter leash than other organizations."

"And are you concerned about something in particular?"

Worry came into his eyes, and he seemed startled when his hand returned with another shrimp.

"There's been some whispering that he could have become a liability. The fear is that if Hew has spun out of control, we want to dissociate the organization from him before our year-end report, and prevent any damage."

A white woman his age approached, looked at my rumpled attire, and then at the man, and he told her, "This is a journalist. He's checking us out."

"Brigitte," she said with a French accent in British English, and extended her hand. "I'm the wife of the rascal you're harassing. What are you writing about?"

"I've been doing some research on conservation," I told her, and mumbled, "about Richmond Hew, and—"

"Richmond Hew? Whatever for?"

"You know Hew?" I asked.

The director closed his eyes and groaned quietly.

"I do indeed," she said. "He facilitated several of our projects years back. He is the one man who stayed out here during the entire war."

"There must be Congolese conservationists—"

She waved her hand.

"It's not the same. You didn't see the destruction, the absolute genocide of the animals. To call it a holocaust would be to put it mildly. And he was out there, single-handedly arming guards and protecting vast swathes of wildlife from poachers. He is a hero, despite whatever shortcomings he may, or may not, have."

"I'm simply looking into some things I've heard," I said.

"Africans will tell you whatever you want to hear."

"Most people will," I replied, "especially when something's at stake for them."

The director finished swallowing some smoked salmon and said, "I bet it's about the girls."

"It is," I said.

"See," he told her, as if I'd simply intruded upon their argument.

"It can't be believed," she said.

A small paper plate of crudités trembled in her fingers.

"I'm just investigating," I replied. "If a man were having sex with underage girls in France—"

"Belgium," she interrupted, "but I get your point."

"Yes, so if this happened in Belgium, wouldn't you want me to investigate?"

"Things are done differently in Africa," she said and strode off, pausing only to throw her plate in the trash, before going outside to stare at the lake as it faded into the dark.

I masked my shock, and the director gave an exasperated but matter-of-fact sigh, as if the difficulty with racism were the marital friction it caused. He shook my hand and said, "There's business I must attend to," before glancing across the room at Oméga with an expression that seemed to convey "job done" or "told you so."

As the director walked to the stage, I tried to understand what had just happened. I was certain he wouldn't go on the record and yet, if he didn't intend to, it made no sense for him to share so much. I felt as if I was being spurred on without being offered any tangible proof.

"Tonight," the director said into the microphone, "we would like to introduce you to someone very special."

He motioned, and the crowd parted to let Oméga join him on the platform.

"As of today, Pastor Thomas Oméga has been appointed—by the president of the Democratic Republic of Congo—the new minister of the environment."

He shook Oméga's hand as the audience applauded. The director introduced him as one who'd led both with his faith and political convictions. He spoke lengthily in the pseudoreligious language of corporate laud—"commemoration," "observation," "gratitude," "honor."

As the audience tapped out their applause, a large woman in a yellow-flowered pagne carried a box onto the stage and stood between Oméga and the director. Reaching from each side, the two men lifted the lid, and three doves flapped out. The woman smiled upward, revealing gapped front teeth, as the confused birds pounded their wings to stay aloft just below the concrete ceiling.

"Congratulations," I told Oméga a little later, as some of the conferees danced on the terrace and the rest jockeyed at the buffet and wine bar. "I'm happy for you."

"Thank you," he said. "I'm sorry for what happened. I've had similar experiences. Enemies who are afraid to strike out at me have targeted my helpers, often robbing them in the process, as a cover-up. But despite our grief, we must focus on the living."

We left the hall and stood outside where we could hear more easily.

"I've arranged for a truck to bring his body back to Goma," he said, "and I will stay to speak at his funeral. Travel in the Congo has always carried risks, but since the wars, violence of this sort is not uncommon, not only because of the rebel groups living in the mountains, but also because of people's desperation."

He glanced at me, and it was the first time I'd seen such strong emotion on his face, clear lines of sadness marking the skin around his eyes and mouth.

"This recalls our earlier conversation, does it not?" he said.

"Which one?"

"Regarding the best seller, and your belief in convictions rising from within."

"Well, yes," I replied, unsure of why he was talking about this now.

"You seemed to hold the conviction that true motivation ignores the externalities that shake and wound us."

I was no longer entirely certain as to what my argument had been and whether I'd overstated my case, as I often did.

"It's not that I think externalities should be entirely excluded," I said. "I can see great storytelling happening somewhere in that intersection between the internal drive of people to see their beliefs mirrored around them and how they react to challenging circumstances—both those that are already in motion in the world, and also those that they set into motion by their convictions."

Oméga took a moment to consider this.

"That is more just," he said. "Where life's fragility is so clear, it's difficult to separate the external from the internal. Of course, I recognize your concern that a story that focuses on externalities can devolve into affirmations of norms. Yet I have since given a good deal of thought to your comment regarding movies in which aliens attack the earth. For those of us living in this country whose history has forced us to bear witness to constant plunder, alien invasion does not sound so strange."

"That makes sense," I said and paused to collect my thoughts. I was very tired and felt as if years of conversations were bleeding into the present. "But America's stories of alien invasion are different," I made myself say, "subjecting it to the sort of military aggression it directs at weaker nations, and yet it wins, usurping others as the underdog even while confirming its myth of superiority."

Oméga nodded appreciatively. "Yes. That's very true. But my problem with such films is not necessarily the concept but the simplicity of that which results. I would like to see a film about an alien invasion that lasts centuries, that forces the people to live like the aliens, think like the aliens, eat like them, fight like them, and even tell stories like them. That would take internal searching—a great effort of memory for the people to recall who they once were and to imagine who they might be in a future in which they are free."

Briefly, I was distracted by the appearance of young Congolese women inside and on the terrace. As they paired off with men, I scanned their faces, wondering if Baraka's beloved was among them and if his death would matter to her.

"In the past," Oméga said, "you have spoken of conviction, but I'm not sure that you've ever named what it is for you."

"I'm working on it," I replied, struggling to quell a sense of regret. "It involves self-questioning, the dismantling of the self that is necessary to create something new."

The music was turned up, and beyond the lights of the bar, the lake was now so dark that the hotel appeared to be perched on a cliff.

We walked slowly toward the door that led to the quiet courtyard.

"A question I have," I said, though uncertain of myself, "is agency. We're in this chaotic world. I guess I want to explore how much I can actually choose."

"Yes, despite my faith, I am the one who believes that we have freedom at each fork in the path—that God gives this to us. But you, if I understand, believe that society and circumstances determine your path, a sort of colorless, spiritless destiny that you must overcome through mental acrobatics so as to liberate yourself. You hoard knowledge and experience, certain that you are meant for something, but not knowing what, yet always ready to make a leap that, in retrospect, appears to have been but a lead up to the leap you were intended to make."

Just off the courtyard, a generator rumbled in a shed. Despite the lights of the hotel, the stars blazed in a long sweep from the volcanoes, blurring in the dense night above the lake's invisible horizon.

Oméga wasn't quite right. Rather, I'd always believed that every experience reflected my importance and pointed toward self-fulfillment. On my travels, I had walked blindly into stillness and felt the liberating emptiness around my life: waking to myself as a mere and unjust social construct before a silent universe. I'd experienced that stillness as peace because, ever so briefly, I was no longer burdened by my significance. But maybe he'd also been right, in our earlier conversation, when he'd said there was a grain of faith in me. If so, it was contorted beyond any normal comprehension of the word, and I was spending my life trying to free myself of it.

"In any case," Oméga told me, "I believe it's time for us to confront the issue of Hew directly. As I once told you, there are formal complaints that village chieftains have sent to the ministry, and it's now my duty to investigate them."

From his pocket, he slipped a single folded sheet of notebook paper. The frail blue of the lines had begun to run and the handwriting on the other side bled through. He spread it out, showing me a simple message written with a ballpoint pen. I made out the writing in French, *We the chiefs of* . . . a list of provincial sectors and administrative divisions followed . . . *accuse Monsieur Richmond Hew of sexually abusing the girls in our villages. We demand that the ministry of the environment remove him from this position as* conservateur, *for the welfare of our families and communities, as well as for the future of the projects that he leads.*

A dozen signatures were below, some in different colors of ink. I suspected the document had been relayed between villages, along sandy trails, before being carried in a jacket pocket for months on dirt roads and slow river barges.

Oméga refolded the paper. We paced the flagstones between flowerbeds as he spoke. From his sources, he'd learned that Hew had left the east and returned to the rainforests in the center of the country. If I wanted the scoop, I'd have to go there quickly, before the independent investigator released his report. But I struggled to follow his words, looking at the night sky, thinking about alien invasions and how much they revealed about white Americans' detachment from history: the empty present we lived in, waiting for the universe to deliver an opportunity for us to triumph yet again.

We'd entered the courtyard, within sight of the exterior gate, when a man began shouting. Oméga and I turned to see three hotel guards arguing.

Two of them held something pale, and the third was pointing, gesticulating, as if on the verge of violence, though he never touched the others—one of whom made a shrugging motion, letting something flutter up from his hands. He'd been holding two of the doves, I realized. The other guard held only one, but the shouting man hadn't had any. He lashed his arm out and snatched the bird from the air, catching its head in a fluid motion, and then swung it like a whip, snapping its neck.

Oméga hardly appeared to notice, and I refused to feel repulsed. I'd been told that many Congolese could afford to eat only once every one or two days. Maybe in the eyes of the sated, hunger too often looks like cruelty.

17

GLINT, BY ALTON HOOKE

The next morning, I called Sola for an update on the girl and to tell her that I was heading off the grid, but I struggled to stay focused, pausing too often to think about Baraka—certain that I had to write about him now—and yet unable to find words to tell her what had happened.

"It's nice that you've been calling," she said. "You're quick to connect."

"I guess that's true," I replied, unsure whether this was a criticism, a compliment, or a simple observation. "It's always seemed to me that two people can spend years together and still not know anything meaningful about each other, or that strangers can . . . you know . . ."

"Sure, but I wonder if you're also quick to disconnect. You sound more interested in the metaphysics of human relationships than in the caring and commitment most people crave."

"That may be," I said, "to some degree at least . . ."

"It's not that one can't be interested in both relationships in the abstract and actual loving relationships," she added, offering me a path out.

I took it, but not very heartily, simply agreeing, and then asked how she'd been otherwise and whether she'd found the girl. She hadn't, and soon she was telling me that she had to run and wished me good luck.

"Good luck to you too," I told her. Maybe our connection wasn't deep enough to merit more intimate words. In truth, I liked her and missed her, but I feared that my emotions would shut off, as if someone—an invisible hand in my past—had flicked a switch.

The next two days merited the sort of travelogue I hate: adventurous white man discovers that no commercial flights are running to the center of the Congo, to the remote town closest to the vast forests where the subject of his inquiry dwells; he bribes passage on a Russian-made and -piloted cargo plane that brings pineapples and cassava from the interior and carries in bundles of plastic chairs and other Chinese factory items; the police and several military officers stop him before he boards, and he negotiates a bribe, displaying his knowledge of how to navigate such situations. It's a formality, he knows. We all bargain with what we have, and his safety is assured by their need to extort enough to survive.

The plane landed on a bumpy stretch of packed, red earth, though the nearby town was built on the deep sand underlying much of the rainforest. The streets were like rutted beaches, with an ancient tree here or there, its roots offering solid ground on which men sat to repair bicycles and electronics.

Though no friends of Omége met me here, plenty of

men offered their services as drivers, translators, and guides. I hired a few, and together we inquired about Richmond Hew and Alton Hooke, but everyone I met—officials, traders, and workers—squinted warily, repeating, "*Un homme blanc . . .*"

I slept that night in an odd, barrack-like concrete structure that passed for a hotel, in whose courtyard two drunk out-of-towners sat up until late with a radio wired to their motorcycle battery, and took turns going into their shared room with a pretty young woman who'd stooped through the low doorway from the street. After the men extinguished their candles and turned off the radio, the night and silence were enveloping.

The next morning, I ducked out of the hotel.

The sun was rising and several streets over, one of the town's few trucks—perhaps its only one, as I had yet to see any four-wheeled vehicles—was revving its engine, its tires spinning, stuck in sand and spouting a high, twisting current of yellow dust: a golden feather above the thatch and tin rooftops.

Nearby, a young man leaned against his motorcycle, his arms crossed. He had a white eye and a scar so deep on his temple that his head was slightly misshapen. He turned, his working eye seeing me, and he approached.

"How much is this worth to you?" he asked in a shy voice. He held up a small manila envelope addressed to and from Alton Hooke, with a Las Vegas address.

"It depends on whether it comes with the story of how you got it."

"For just the envelope, two hundred dollars. For the envelope and my story, three hundred."

I widened my eyes in mock surprise.

"No way," I said. "Who can waste that kind of money on an envelope?"

He blinked, turned partially away and then back, and I almost felt sorry for him, realizing that he might not be used to playing this game, having simply known he should start with a high price. A negotiation followed and we settled on $40 for the package, $60 with his story, keeping to his ratio.

The package contained a mini flash drive, and the young man—his name was Jules—told me in his hushed voice that a white foreigner had come into town looking haggard and feverish. He'd tried to find a post office. When he realized that one didn't exist here, he offered to hire local officials and chiefs to ship the package. He paid the highest bidder, who, having no means of getting it to Las Vegas, kept it and eventually sent it via Jules, to sell to me.

"You will deliver it?" he asked, as if I'd just paid for that duty.

"Of course," I told him. "And where did this white man go afterward?"

"Into the forest north of here. I heard he was staying at a hotel on the national highway."

"The national highway?"

Jules pointed to the side, into the distance.

"And what is the name of the hotel?"

"There is no name. It used to be a plantation on the river. Now it's forest."

I asked how to get there, and he offered to drive. Though his blind eye worried me, I agreed, telling myself he'd survived on his motorcycle so far.

When I returned with my bag, four young men came running, and he tried to shoo them away.

"What do they want?" I asked.

The young men were holding up battered and soiled envelopes, old documents, even zip drives.

"They have documents left by white men."

"Are any from Alton Hooke or Richmond Hew?"

I inspected them, but none were, and since I showed little interest, I was able to negotiate a price of a few dollars for each of the lost records.

The national highway turned out to be a long, winding groove of sand through mud-and-wattle villages and scattered forest that occasionally opened out on the vast rolling landscapes of the savannah: tall grass, scattered trees, the slanted earth neither hill nor mountain, but something like steppes—a gathering of inclines.

The hotel we arrived at that night was a Belgian mansion from the colonial period, its concrete falling away in places to show the large red bricks beneath.

The owner, Serge—a hunched old man with a potbelly and a petite younger wife named Aimée—showed me a room empty but for an antique bed with a scrolled headboard, a foam mattress, and a mosquito net. He told me that they might be able to find and cook some goat entrails and rice for dinner if I could pay them now. I specified that the stomach and liver would be fine, along with rice and some greens if possible, but not the intestines, and they agreed.

Jules departed, saying that he had to get the motorcycle back to his uncle. I washed up, returned to my room, and lay on the bed, under the mosquito net, with my laptop. I plugged in Hooke's flash drive and opened the single document it contained.

GLINT, by Alton Hooke

The Congo. The great river. Coiled around the heart of Africa—the land of treasure, the forbidden fruit. I've fantasized about it since I was a boy. The first time I looked at a lingerie catalogue, I stared at the lacy crotch, where what I wanted had been airbrushed away. That's how I felt seeing the Congo on a map. Conrad was right about the allure of blank spaces.

I dreamed of how I'd get here. Special forces. Foreign Legion. Or just a mercenary. But Dad demanded that I go into finance. The military, he said, was for people who lacked options. This is why I've been so reckless, why—even after the car accident and my parents' funeral—especially after—I burned through my options, financial or otherwise. Parties, lines of coke on shaved pubes, gambling, exotic firearm parties in the desert. Grendels, Kel-Tecs, Tavors, Steyrs, Colt Defender Mark I 8-barreled shot guns, and of course Desert Eagles. We fired exploding bullets at photocopied photos of the president taped to husks of old cars, to empty beer bottles. Yes, We Can. *That's how I burned it all down to the one last option: the beach house my sister and I inherited—two million dollars of salt-eaten clapboards facing a slab of sand in Nantucket.*

Madison and I hardly spoke. When I'd paid to have my DNA sequenced—Norseman via England, a bit of French and Celtic, with a mysterious dash of Slav—I told her, and she asked to see it, said she'd do the same, only to admit she'd done so with the sole hope of discovering that we didn't share the same father, that one of us had been the fruit of infidelity. No such luck.

If I'd asked her to meet me at the beach house, she'd have flown to Paris, but I knew she'd be there. It was her favorite time of year—late summer, already cool, the ex-presidents and senators and future SCOTUS types all returned to the Hill.

I parked my rental SUV on the gravel. The same tan bikini she'd worn since high school hung on the line, along with a threadbare towel showing a woman bicycling in the wind.

I snooped through the house. She wasn't in, but her bed was made, a stack of books next to it: bell hooks, Irigaray, Judith Butler. She was probably brushing up to brainwash another generation of young women into misery.

The wood creaked like the hull of a ship as I walked back to my childhood room. The baseball banners. A model frigate. Junk I'd hated but pretended to enjoy for Dad's pleasure, when all I wanted was to blow shit up or get shot at.

I hadn't been back here since our parents' deaths. A lot had been cleaned up. Fair enough. Madison used it. I'd never cared, not until now, when I'd cleared out my accounts and was on my beam's end.

Propping the window open was a foxed, coverless novel, and I flopped onto the bed and started reading. There was no title page either, but the name and author were printed in the upper corners: Twice Dead, *by Willard Calhoun.*

The opening had me instantly. A police detective receives an envelope containing only a map into the desert outside Reno. He's been investigating the death of two strippers, maybe a suicide pact, maybe a double homicide.

He's getting off work, considering he might patch things up with his wife, but she tells him he calls only when he wants ass, and he realizes it's true. He's turned on from spending a day staring at the murder-scene photos of the strippers. She tells him to fuck off.

He's halfway to the bar when he catches himself, doesn't want to fall off the wagon, and figures what the hell and drives into the desert. The afternoon is cooling fast. He's brought a jacket, but he's still cold, and then he comes to the cave, the X on the map between two long, spreading ridges.

His footsteps echo. The air inside is chill, as if this were somewhere far north.

Even before his eyes adjust, he can see her glow, the naked girl reclining in a crystalline subterranean pool. Slender limbs, small, hard breasts, long blond hair. The Lady of the Lake, but stone-cold dead, her beauty preserved by the frigid water.

He spends a little time, just looking at her, afraid to touch her, forgetting to be afraid that he might not be alone, before he calls her in.

But he can't stop picturing her—her stillness, her perfection, her beauty—and later that night, he thinks he sees her watching him from a street corner. He begins glimpsing her around town, always in the evening, her long, pale figure always at the edge of sight, the unmistakable legs, the enticing throat and high, delicate neck of a runway model.

— Oh, for crying out loud, my sister said from the door. That fucking book!

—Hey! What? I pulled up my knee to hide the bulge of my partial erection.

— Don't get too attached to it. I tore the ending off and composted it.

— It's just a story, I told her, not wanting to start a fight, not now, when I needed to convince her to sell this place or buy my share.

— Oh, she said, let me guess, you were totally turned on by the hot dead chick who begins mysteriously following the detective around and then reappears in the flesh and screws him, turning out to be—what a surprise!—the twin sister of the murdered girl. The detective escapes the shrew he's been trying to divorce for, like, ever, to find joy in the arms of a sensuous girl he isn't quite sure is really alive, except that it turns out that she's not really asking for his protection or trying to help him solve her sister's murder, but is trying to lead him astray and was complicit in it, her own twin's murder, so that—big shock—in the end of the book, he shoots and kills her. Lots of Lilith and Eve imagery, and a sense that the first murderer wasn't Cain but Adam, when he had to deal with the first bitch. So what does the detective get out of all the heartbreak? A racy, pedo-erotic fling with a nubile girl who isn't fully of this world and so isn't consequential, and because she's evil, he can fuck her and kill her. It's like getting free dinner because there's a hair in your soup. He gets to fuck a soulless Snow White or Sleeping Beauty or whatever for a month, guilt- and responsibility-free. And then his wife suddenly spruces herself up, and he's happy to be home.

I quote her verbatim. This is how she talked, a PhD in cultural studies, a professor at a school for lesbians. She didn't believe in the Y chromosome or testosterone. Such things were cultural articulations of patriarchal hegemony. A throbbing cock? All in the eye of the beholder. Could be an olive branch. A teddy bear. A hand massager.

— You just ruined it for me, I told her, hoping to leverage a little guilt.

— Porn can't be ruined by a spoiler, she said. That book's the pulp-fiction equivalent of a money shot.

She stuck out her tongue and waggled her fingers in front of her chin.

— All. Over. Her. Face.

I had no idea what in the hell she was talking about, except for the part about the money shot, which was kind of hot, even though she was my sister.

— Anyway, I said, you read the whole thing. It couldn't have been that bad.

— I read it when I was twelve. That fucking book has been in my head for years. Traumatized me. Made me think I would be most attractive to men if I died right when I hit puberty and left my legs spread just in time for rigor mortis.

— Come on. It's just a book.

— So's the Bible, and look at its body count.

— Well, this book isn't that bad.

— No, modern patriarchal narrative takes women down with teamwork. Thousands and thousands of books. A million whispering voices telling us that men only want to fuck us and kill us, not necessarily in that order.

— This is why you're still single, you know.

— Actually, I have a partner.

— Does this partner have tits?

— Not when they're exercising.

— You have multiple partners?

— Not "they," "xe." I refer to xem with a gender-neutral pronoun.

— Oh Christ.

— Never mind.

She was right. I did want to kill her. I wanted to kill the entire liberal culture. I wanted to feel the vein in my bicep bulge as I held my rifle in the crook of my arm, a posture I'd fantasized about since owning my first G.I. Joe, the way the little black rifle snapped into place, the plastic soldier's swaggering stance. If she were dead, I could sell this fucking firetrap of a beach house. If my memories of it and of its effete, blue-blooded neighbors had any value, I'd hawk them on eBay.

I'd been gearing up for a fight, but when I followed her into the main room, she put two mugs on the table and poured hot water over mint tea bags. The sun had burst like an atomic paintball over the ocean.

— So what do you want? she asked.

— Huh? Say what?

— Don't bullshit me. For a guy who likes detective stories, you're not reading your own clues too well.

So I told her—that I'd been through intense times since the death of our parents, that I was down to my last few G's, and I had plans to start over, to begin an eco-adventure tourism company in Africa, that I'd met a former Navy SEAL when he'd been leading survivalist courses in Wyoming.

— I'm not selling this place, ever, she said, but of course I'd love to buy you out, so long as you promise never to visit.

— So, uh, can you do a million?

—I'm not rich.

—What happened to your half of the inheritance?

—Yah. I've squirreled some of that away, but I also bought a condo in Manhattan for weekends, when I take the train into the city. It's a professional investment. Networking. But at the end of the day, I'm a university professor. I don't earn much.

Regardless, we came up with a price—not a clean million, which was half of what the place was listed for on Zillow.com, though its evaluation probably hadn't been updated in a decade. People would pay just for the social privileges. The DNA of every Washington insider could be swabbed off the toilet bowl at the lobster shack.

I didn't expect her to understand. She and I were like those distant primeval ancestors of humans and chimpanzees, two siblings from the same mother, wandering off to give rise to two vastly different species.

I couldn't say which of us was speciating right then. Maybe both of us. Though I hated where her lineage was headed, I didn't care for mine either. My generation, or at least my generation of my class, didn't get real war and rape, but the figurative war and rape of financial markets. Per capita, we made off with more homes and family fortunes than Genghis Khan. We even got the daughters of those vanquished by globalization—Eastern Europeans, Laotians, Venezuelans—the girls here, among us, desperate to survive, lounging in clubs, on VIP sites to be ordered over for an hour with a few clicks. These weren't even the Midwestern girls we seduced with drinks or dinner. No respect was involved. They were etymologically classic, right out of Middle English: booty in the purest sense of the word.

Someone was calling to me. It was Aimée, the diminutive wife of the hotel owner. She was outside my door, saying that dinner was ready.

The large main room was empty but for a table. Two candles burned on it, a few mosquitoes floating past them, casting flimsy shadows. A single plate was set next to three battered tin pots. I spooned out rice and then the chopped-up liver and stomach stewed in palm oil, as well as a clump of mysterious greens.

Serge shuffled into the kitchen to speak to her. I knew I should interview them, but reading Hooke had been draining, and at that moment I had humanity fatigue. I was too exhausted to acknowledge their stories, which would be (considering his age and that he'd lived through the end of Belgian colonialism, the upheaval during Independence, the massacres, migrations, and ideological conflict of the Congo Crisis, the rise of Mobutu's dictatorship, the collapse of the national infrastructure, and the two recent wars) certain to be long and, without doubt, compelling and painful.

After eating, I thanked Aimée and returned to my room. I lay on the foam mattress, bothered that Hooke's ugliness had made me feel like a shining example of the sensitive male, and yet he and I had clearly grown up reading the same stories, fantasizing similar freedoms. It wasn't that I identified with him but rather that I'd been raised to identify with a type of man depicted by the masculine authors I'd loved as a boy. Their muscular language, the assuredness with which they spoke of violence they'd never experienced, their casual understatement of horror—all this had also been performance, not unlike the usual social role-playing I so disliked.

The sun had set, and there was a density to the rainforest

night. I'd experienced it before—an absence of electrical disturbance, all sounds absorbed by the resonance of nocturnal creatures. It pinned me in place, and when I closed my eyes to think, I was instantly asleep. The images that came to me—the misted river and my father, but also a teenage girl of whom I almost never spoke and whom, even now, I still pictured as a woman—were more memories than dreams.

Gradually, I sensed a presence at the window, the outline of a figure who—when the descending moon shone past the trees—faded away, just as I had from the dreams into which I stared, so that I had the impression I was both the body dreaming and the man outside the glass watching me dream, seeing me wake, and then retreating from the window, as I receded from my dreams as I woke.

When I came to again, the sun was high. My jaw was sore from clenching my teeth, and I was so hot and sweaty that I feared I was getting sick.

I took my toiletry bag and walked outside, behind the hotel, to where a rusted pipe protruded from a hillside, gushing spring water into a concrete basin that drained down steep fields grown to shrubby forest, and emptied into a river.

Hundreds of white butterflies gathered on the soap suds from an earlier wash, pulsing their wings, and as I lathered my face, massaging my jaw muscles, they clouded up. Their tiny bodies, in such great numbers, shaded me from the sun.

Looking up at them, I was a young man again, standing beneath a street lamp at night, dreaming of distance and the character I would become, as snowflakes swarmed down past the high, yellow glass, stinging my cheeks.

Maybe stories hadn't saved me after all.

18

GLINT: NOTES FOR THE SCREENPLAY

Inside the Belgian mansion, dust motes hung in the air, making the angles of shadow and light palpable and brilliant.

By the time I'd returned to my room, I was certain that I was getting sick. Maybe the Pentus hadn't worked. Or maybe I was coming down with yellow fever. I'd been vaccinated, but you could never be sure that you were protected from all strains.

I lay beneath the mosquito net, observing my rising temperature, the way the heat moved in slow swells through my body and flashed beneath my skin.

When I opened my eyes again, Serge stood in the doorway. He offered to make me eggs and rice, and though I wasn't hungry, I agreed, knowing I should eat. Then I went through my first aid kit and started a treatment for malaria.

I opened my laptop and continued to read Hooke's novel, which soon devolved into scattered notes, followed by a reflection on how few people read books and on the death of the novel—how film was the medium of our day.

He then started his story over as a screenplay.

GLINT

These are the adventures of Alt Lockhart, the scion of a wealthy Boston family . . .

Camera pans. Dense forest canopy. A path between immense tree trunks. Fire ants pour across it like blood. Fade to actual blood flowing from a dead man's nostrils. His eyes are half open, their whites bright in the shadow.

ALT (V.O.)

It all began at a Las Vegas electronics fair. That's where I met Kip, a former Navy SEAL. He went to the fair to find the best GPS and navigation equipment, high-tech, low-weight tools that might make the difference between life and death in the jungles.

Cut to Kip. We recognize him as the dead man, though he's alive--tall and raw-boned but strong, with a black mustache and pockmarked cheeks. He stares at the camera, just seeing, appraising coldly. The emotional part was already dead.

Kip leads Alt through glinting rows of electronics.

KIP (speaking back over his shoulder)

None of this works without tantalum. You want tantalum, you walk into the Congo with a bag of cash--not even that much, say, ten grand. You go in and there are dealers. But if you wanted--if you're the kind of man who believes that he who eats the burger must be willing to slaughter the cow--you could hire a militia. Young men on drugs. Stealing. Raping. Torturing. They go into a village and round up some people, and get them digging in the streams. That's how easy tantalum is. No fancy mines or equipment. It comes up as coltan, which is a dull metal--an amalgam of columbite and tantalite that gets refined to tantalum, named after Tantalus, a villain in Greek mythology, one of those guys who was always stealing secrets and treasures from the gods. Anyway, tantalum substitutes for platinum in capacitors.

Every laptop, handheld, and game
console in this place needs it.
But lest we get distracted, they
also need copper, cobalt, and
sometimes gold, and those are
also in the Congo. Sometimes,
when you're bringing out one
thing, a man asks if you want
another. Maybe a bag of gold.
Maybe some of the diamonds that
aren't industrial grade. Big
stones, some even with good
colors, rarities that probably
took a few lives on their way to
reaching you.

ALT (V.O.)

Kip had a front, an ecotour
company that smuggled out
discrete quantities of diamonds.
But he didn't need me. So I had
to show him my worth. I invited
him to play paintball in the
Nevada desert with five fashion
models I'd met at a finance
party.

Cut to Nevada desert. Five slim women in cyberpunk outfits lather up with sunblock. In combat boots, they swagger between the sage and cacti, toting high-powered rifles, wearing sleek goggles. Pan to Alt and Kip. We see Kip smile for the first time as he tracks one of the girls into an arroyo. He fires. Red paint splatters across her goggles and she falls, twisted seductively, her black leather skirt riding high on her thigh.

ALT (V.O.)

So I was in. We set up Cormac Meridians Inc. and began working on how to get minerals out of the Congo. But there was one other person involved, a man so frightening that I didn't realize until I met him Kip's true reason for letting me sign on. He wanted backup. No, he wanted someone to sacrifice--to leave behind him if he had to escape. We called the man the Keeper. His eyes were as pale as cataracts. He was big, grungy, like a farmer, except he'd come to the rainforest to protect the animals. If he caught men poaching, he killed them.

Cut to large white man standing amid burning huts, with a torch in one hand and a machete in the other, a hunting rifle slung across his back. His chloral blue eyes bore into the camera.

ALT (V.O.)

```
For a man who preferred
isolation, the Keeper talked
a lot. Kip told me that when
prisoners were released from
solitary confinement, they
jabbered incessantly. We're
social animals, and the brain
will converse with itself if it
must. I saw this manic need to
communicate--to give his reasons
to the world and justify them--
in the Keeper. I heard rumors of
how he handled problems: a young
Irish woman who tried to make her
own nature reserve on his land or
an outside investigator sent by a
conservation organization.
```

My fever suddenly reversed itself, and I began shivering. I no longer felt fit to write anything about the Congo, or knew why I had gone so far from the unresolved mythological landscape of my childhood to this one.

I wanted to stop, to sleep and wake with a clearer, more robust and healing view of the world, but I needed clues, even if they came from Hooke.

```
Cut to Keeper sitting on a log, holding
a three-foot piece of rebar. The con-
servation investigator, a gray-haired
Canadian man, lies on the ground, his
hands and feet tied.
```

INVESTIGATOR

You're going to do it with that?

THE KEEPER

If it's any consolation, a piece of rebar out here is worth a lot . . .

My joints and lumbar ached, and I blinked so slowly that I lost track of time.

Eventually, I went back to scanning the document. Something about it—beyond the clear egregiousness—troubled me. It took me a moment to realize what it was. Hooke was invisible in it. He was the watcher in the way that often made protagonists seem absent, allowing space for the audience to stand and see through them.

His screenplay would purify his narrator into the ultimate *homme blanc* on his exotic adventures, a blank character the audience could inhabit, who, no matter his mistakes, would be a *blanc*ness on which we write our stories of innocence and superiority—both victim of savagery and its conqueror.

Cut to a boy stalking through the forest with a filthy Kalashnikov. His eyes and skin shine. He has been birthed in violence, nursed by it, and comes as its emissary. He nears a clearing where three white men and a Tutsi commander stand around a synthetic sisal sack of diamonds that they've just removed from a hole. They spin to face him as the boy fires. Kip falls. In the boy's eyes, we see the men reflected, the muzzles of their guns sparking.

I stretched out, breathing deeply. Static crepitated around my head, and I felt the distance from this landscape to the places I once knew, as if taut, invisible lines trembled between me and my old selves.

When I opened my eyes again, the light through the dirty windows burned at a new angle in the dust-laden air, and—as if briefly inhabiting the shadow of another's body—I knew that Hooke had lain here, writing the words I'd read.

I eased myself off the mattress and stepped slowly down the hallway.

Breakfast was on the table, the dishes lidded and covered with cloths, and just outside the door, on the porch, Serge and Aimée stood talking to a girl. She couldn't have been older than thirteen and wore a red dress and new flat-soled sandals whose bands were inset with clear plastic jewels. A red scarf, tied around her head, hid her hair.

All three of them looked startled by my appearance. Serge motioned to her, saying, with an air of guilt, "This is our daughter."

The girl stepped backward off the porch with the elegance of a ballerina, lowering her toes to touch the stairs. She seemed to hover on the balls of her feet as her mother murmured in a language I didn't know and the girl responded with a few hushed phrases. Then she was down the steps, following a thin path into the forest.

"She doesn't live here?" I asked.

"Sometimes, yes, but sometimes she stays with relatives,

helping them. There is much to be done elsewhere, and life has been quiet in the hotel."

I wanted to ask about the girl's new clothes, the obvious indulgence amid the poverty here. It was matched by nothing else in the hotel.

"Your breakfast is ready," Serge said. "I didn't want to wake you."

"It's okay," I told him, "but I was wondering . . . I heard that there was a man here named Alton Hooke."

He looked down and nodded slowly.

"Monsieur Alton, yes. He was here but has been gone for some time now."

"Did he have a fever too?"

"Yes, he was not well."

"And do you know of a man named Richmond Hew?"

Serge shook his head. "I do not."

He motioned me to the table.

I sat, convinced he was lying, suspicious of and fearful for his daughter, recalling her determined stride into the forest, like a Little Red Riding Hood setting off to find her wolf. I touched my plate, uncertain as to whether I could eat.

Serge was watching me with consternation, deep lines on his forehead.

"Is there a problem?" I asked.

"There is something else."

"Tell me."

"One of the tribes has cut down trees to block the road in both directions. They are angry that you are here without their permission. They don't like *mundele*. Their memories of colonialism are strong. They will send someone to speak to you."

"Do they want money?"

"They want to know why you're on their land. When

white men come, the forests get cut down. The earth gets dug up. They want to protect their way of life."

"But I'm a journalist."

"Many visitors say that, and then the machinery shows up."

I couldn't eat after all. I had no appetite and my tongue felt like the swollen edge of a wet towel. Staggering back to the bed required such exertion that my hands and feet went numb. A cold, greasy sweat beaded on my forehead.

Dreading my fading strength, I felt the growing urge to do something, however small or symbolic, to remind myself of purpose. I recalled Oméga's comment about my "pity for the superstitious savage" and my ensuing realization of all I'd never written about the American South, where I'd moved when I was ten and lived for years—how I'd been trained by white friends, teachers, the men who hired me to mow their lawns, the farmers I worked for on weekends, all of them warning me to fear black people, telling me repeatedly why I couldn't be their friends, why I shouldn't see them as equals. In my elementary and middle school, white boys and black boys threatened each other and fought. In high school, during the Rodney King riots, a white boy spray-painted LAPD #1 on the school rock, a boulder on which there was normally an image of a falcon—the school's mascot.†

---

† Editor's note: Béchard inserted the text that follows into the unfinished manuscript that he assembled from his journals and interviews, and left on the desk in his hotel room.

As a child living in the rural South, I was confused as to why white people—with the passion of injured honor—spoke of the War of Northern Aggression, of the harm done to their families and communities, and the destruction wrought on their lands, but almost never of slavery. Black hardship—on the rare occasions that whites spoke of it—was discussed as if it were divorced from history, not as a contextual trait but an essential one, an innate quality of blackness rather than the consequence of violence and oppression.

Hooke's film would do the same, making war in Africa seem not a consequence but an inevitability. With violence portrayed as an animal attribute, blackness is reduced to simple mechanistic nature. Hooke's film would be yet another colonial story not of man versus another's society, but man versus nature, in which nature confronts the white man, but does so with a black face—thus justifying the white fantasy of colonization. Not only must land be conquered and worked, but the emissaries of nature must be tamed and made to labor it.

*Here, I think of the Lithuanian-born Jewish philosopher, Emmanuel Levinas, who, in an interview about his theory of the face as ethical imperative, stated: "The face is not in front of me (*en face de moi*) but above me; it is the other before death, looking through and exposing death. Secondly, the face is the other who asks me not to let him die alone, as if to do so were to become an accomplice in his death. Thus the face says to me: you shall not kill."*

Not acknowledging the humanity in a face requires a laborious societal act of rewriting, of overlaying, of transforming the face into a signifier. The dehumanized face can then, against its will, be put to service in the stories of whites. The violence of whiteness is in the word itself—the semantic purity that allows us to commit horrors while seeing ourselves as innocent.

In Virginia, I'd felt I was nobody, my identity absent, coalescing in opposition to what it was not, before evaporating into the self's easeful forgetting that is both absolution and absoluteness, a way of being as present and unquestionable as air. Here, in the Congo, I knew I was un homme blanc. *I drifted through landscape tableaus, carried by the efforts of others, as if on a litter.*

I would find a way to write all of this, but for now, I needed to focus on recovering. The fever rose and fell, heat followed by chills, but in the moments between, there was something cleansing about the illness. All other preoccupations fell away, and I was just a body, on the earth, emptied of beliefs, listening inside myself for vitality, for the promise of survival.

19

THE RIVER

Mist woke me, clouding about the windows, thinner inside—a cold haze. My windbreaker lay nearby, and I pulled it on.

I was fairly certain it was time for my dose of Pentus, and I washed one down with water that tasted of iodine. I was afraid to go off it, though my fever might not even have been malaria. It reverberated through my skull in waves—a hot resonance, like that of an immense gong, before contracting into the visionless silence of chills.

Lying on the humid mattress, trying to think of how I would get from where I was now to Hew, I had a deep sense of unease—of the unappeasable need to take action. As a child, I'd felt this helplessness during my father's rages, when I'd crossed the fields behind our house and sat alone and read. I'd wanted to go farther, but I'd known even then the frailty of the body and the relentlessness of winter.

We lived in British Columbia, and the settings of his childhood—three thousand miles away—were familiar to me only through books: Québec, named for the Algonquin word *kébec*—“where the river narrows”—referring to the stretch of the Saint Lawrence where the French built Québec City; and the Gaspé Peninsula, its name taken from the Micmac word *gespeg*—“the end of the earth”—the place where the ancient, glacier-carved spine of the Appalachians runs into the sea.

His stories were of a youth without electricity or running water, with little education, days spent cod fishing with his father or harvesting potatoes. He said that French Canadians had been second-class citizens and he’d grown up envying the wealth of English Canadians. He told me that Québec was poor and backwards and there was no point returning. He refused to speak the names of his parents.

Only in the years leading up to his death did he describe how he’d left home young and burned away his late teens and twenties as a criminal, safecracking and pulling armed robberies. By the time he was thirty, he’d spent seven years in prison and had been deported by the US to British Columbia, where he’d met my mother.

She’d given up on the United States because of the war in Vietnam, had considered the modern world corrupt, doomed for collapse, and nurtured a dream of living off the land. She read the publications of the bourgeoning New Age movement, believed in spirit guides and past life regression. The allure of new beginnings in those writings also existed in my father, who’d rejected societal norms and reinvented himself over and over, and who, having grown up poor in rural Quebec, had the skills to fulfill her pastoral dream. Isolated in the rainy valley where we lived, with few neighbors and no extended family, I listened to their words, sensing the possibility of change, the power of intention, and I saw how my mother drew strength from her books and spiritual activities, finding not just community but authority in knowledge.

Her own father had warned her never to marry a Catholic—the possibility of her dating a black man then being too inconceivable to prohibit—and so my father may also have been a means of rebellion, of erotic transgression: a dark, handsome French Canadian, his "darkness" a romantic descriptor left over from an earlier otherness that preceded America's dissolving racial boundaries between whites.

Eventually, my mother found herself unable to tolerate his rages, his threats, and the restrictions he tried to exert on her life. She'd become confident and had seen the self she wanted to be in her books on how to assume her potential and find her place in the world. She'd fled with me to Virginia, craving the freedom he'd allowed only himself.

When I was fourteen, she told me about his criminal past. Being a teenage boy, I was, of course, thrilled. I decided to return to live with him and she eventually accepted my choice.

The man I met in Vancouver, shortly before my fifteenth birthday, was darker than I recalled—his hair, his eyes, even the faint hue of his skin—as if my years in America had changed how I saw him. In person, his accent seemed thicker. Awkwardly, we stood in the airport, staring out the window, watching a plane land, as if we were still waiting for someone to arrive.

When he took me to see his seafood stores, he said he was proud to have recovered from bankruptcy. He described his struggles: being nearly homeless, living out of a van.

My disappointment at the normality of his current life must have been clearer to him than I realized, and as I spent most of my time reading books, his hostility grew. He resented me for the five years I'd been gone, when I'd rarely called him or answered his letters. And now that we were together again, he pressured me to forget about school. Eventually, he had me work at a ferry landing outside the city, where he'd bought a snack bar. Jasmine, a young woman he knew, had been running it. I would help her serve ferry passengers while living with her in a tiny, run-down house.

Now, exhausted by fever, I couldn't help but remember. I lay for hours in the dark, my brain no longer needing delirium.

When I felt strong enough to sit up in bed, I took my laptop and wrote.

> *Each morning, I woke on the couch and walked along the gravel driveway to stand at the ferry docks. It had been four days since I'd seen my father. The breadth of the river registered in my body with a somatic awareness of a boundary. It provoked my mind, the way that a glimpse of a distant peak reminded me of how little I knew about the landscape around me.*
>
> *On one of these mornings, when I went back inside, Jasmine was in the kitchen, making eggs. She wore only a pale nightgown that accentuated her olive skin. Her hair was long, as dark as her eyes and lashes. Her body reminded me of the cheerleaders at my old high school, who, with their womanly hips and breasts and confidence, made me feel as if I were still a child.*
>
> *"Are you going to help me in the snack bar or just read books all day?" she asked.*
>
> *"I'd rather read."*
>
> *"If you want to, I won't tell André, but it would be nice to have your company."*

She put a plate with two fried eggs on the table for me, with some toast. I sat and ate automatically, not waiting for her to prepare her own plate. I mopped up the yolks with torn bread, and then stood and went into the chilly bathroom, where I undressed and showered.

When I came out, she was in the snack bar. I lay on the couch across from the front window, rereading East of Eden. *Falling rain turned to ice, dimming the world outside and creating thin, serried icicles along eaves and power lines. The faint light through the clouds seemed even more diminished. In the row of cars waiting for the ferry, only a few motors ran. There were no customers at the snack bar's counter.*

Jasmine was in the kitchen when I woke. Glasses clinked, and she came into the living room with two lowballs of vodka and orange juice. She gave me one and then knelt before a cardboard box on the floor in the corner, next to a small Christmas tree. She began taking ornaments and strings of lights from the box.

"André dropped this off last time he visited," she told me.

"I don't understand why you stay here."

"It's a job." She put her glass on the floor and began untangling a string of lights, holding it up with one hand while the fingers of the other glided along it, releasing the kinks and knots.

"But isn't there anything else you want to do?"

"I don't know. I guess." The motion of her hand faltered slightly, as if she were suddenly uncertain.

"How do you know my father?"

"He helped me. He used to rent a room from my mom and stepdad. I guess it was after he went bankrupt.

He had an old van and had been living in it and saw an ad for the room somewhere. He was nice to me. My parents drank a lot and got in fights, and I would go and sit with him and he'd tell me about his life and all of the places he'd traveled, and how, after your mother had left him, he'd gone bankrupt. He'd been too heartbroken and hadn't been able to keep up his store."

I hesitated, trying to ignore my father's revised version of the past, since even as a child I'd known that he spent money heedlessly. What bothered me was that he went bankrupt five years earlier and she looked too young for him to have been confiding in her at that time.

"How old were you?" I asked.

She draped the string of lights on the tree.

"Eighteen," she said.

"Really? So you're like twenty-three now?"

"Twenty-two. Anyway, one night, my stepfather got drunk and tried to rape me. When I woke up, he had his hand in my underwear. I screamed, but he . . ."

She stopped speaking, just staring at the tree. She crouched and plugged the string of lights into the wall, and it came alive, flashing.

Silently now, she dressed the tree with bulbs crusted with glitter, shreds of tinsels, and two more strands of lights. It didn't take long. She picked up her glass and came over to the couch. She lifted my ankles and sat in their place, resting my feet on her thighs. The point where we touched felt electric, and I had the impression that if I looked there, I would see a kindling radiance.

"It's nice, isn't it?" she said, staring at the tree.

"Yeah, sure," I told her. "You did a good job."

"You think so?"

"Yeah." We were silent a moment, and I asked, "So what happened?"

"He didn't rape me. My mom came in and . . . and later André offered to let me live with him. He'd found a house to rent. He was selling Christmas trees and seafood again, and he was making some money. My mom didn't want to leave my stepfather, so she agreed. Your father helped me get jobs. And then he got me this place, and he lets me run it."

Outside, the light at the entrance to the ferry docks changed, the glow in the mist shifting from red to green. The wheels of cars clanged over metal.

"I guess it's time for bed," she told me. "Good night."

I moved my feet, and she stood and went upstairs.

The heater had come on, and warm air blew in the vents, failing to dissipate the cold that emanated from the walls and windows.

I shut my eyes, again aware of the immense river just outside. The ceiling creaked, and now I sensed her every movement in her tiny attic room, as if desire propelled my nervous system through my skin and the couch, into the rotting walls.

I closed my laptop and eased away from the headboard, shifting into a lying position.

The Fraser River had no history in my eyes when I was boy. It was a broad expanse, a mere separation, cold and inhospitable, braved by ferries and tugs pulling barges of timber from the province's interior. At the crossing, the river was two thousand feet wide, though in other areas it was over three thousand. Spanish explorers entered the river in 1792, followed shortly by the British, who mapped the shores long inhabited by indigenous communities.

My father told me stories about the river's great floods, the broken log booms releasing thousands of battering rams, and of the drowned men, the capsized boats, the accidents in the fog.

The rain let up, and I left the house and stood at a break in the trees. The shore below was mud and gravel, dead weeds beneath the ice edging the wide, choppy river.

I walked to the snack bar and helped Jasmine for a few hours. She asked how my father was doing and whether he had a girlfriend, and I told her about a thin blond who drove his extra car, who worked for him and whom I thought he might be dating, though I wasn't sure. She was only eighteen, had recently dropped out of high school, and he'd never made clear to me the nature of their relationship.

The ferry line was gone. I went to the house and lay on the couch with my book.

It was dark when I woke, windy and rainy. The string of colored lights in front of the snack bar jerked with each gust. It blinked off. Footsteps climbed the stairs, and Jasmine came inside with the money drawer from the till and put it on the table.

She crouched to plug in the Christmas tree and then stood and said softly, to herself, "There. That's better."

She returned to the kitchen and, as if it were easier to speak to me without seeing me, she called, "I ordered a pizza."

Even though I knew it was coming, when I heard

the gravel outside crunch beneath the delivery car's small tires, my heart sped up.

The house filled with the scent of crust and cheese, and I folded two slices together and then returned to the couch, lying as I read with the plate on my chest.

She went upstairs and then returned. A cassette clicked into the small radio. The sound of her pressing the play button—a loud clack—and the faint squealing of the spindles turning was followed by blaring guitar and drums.

She came into the living room in her nightgown. Its worn straps hung against her collarbone and the ruffled front sagged so that, as she sat, I could discern the movement of her breasts.

She'd brought me another slice of pizza on her plate, as well as one for her, and was holding two glasses of vodka and orange juice in one hand, like a waitress.

I put the book down, and we ate and drank.

"I'm bored," she said and looked at me. I just shrugged.

"Do you want to dance?" she asked.

The song had changed on the mixed tape, to one by Whitesnake. It started with strumming and low singing, but I knew it would get loud and fast soon, and I wasn't sure how we'd be able to dance to that.

We got up, and as the singer's voice rumbled slowly about not knowing where he was going and not wasting any more time, I put my hands on her hips and she put hers on my biceps. We moved like that, side to side, as if at a school dance. The music paused ever so briefly and then the band began to jam, and she slipped my arms over her shoulders and rested her head against my chest, so that we weren't really dancing anymore. I'd seen her as far more mature than I was, but now, with her head nestled beneath my chin and her eyes closed, I had the impression that I was holding someone much younger, and that I was somehow comforting her.

We stood like that, in the middle of the living room, in front of the threadbare curtains, until the next song began, and I asked, very softly, the way I thought it was supposed to be done, "Do you want to make love?"

She nodded, moving her face against my neck and kissing it. Then she let go of me and began pulling the cushions off the couch and aligning them on the floor. She helped me take off my shirt. We lay down and finished undressing.

We kissed. I was above her. She was holding me, and then she froze.

"What?"

"I feel like it's watching," she said.

I followed her gaze to the Christmas tree propped crookedly in the corner.

"We can go upstairs," I told her.

"I don't want to. Just unplug it."

I lifted myself from her, crawled across the floor, and pulled out the plug.

I put my laptop aside. The sun had set, and with dusk, my fever reignited. I lay, drifting between sleep and dreams and thought, until the generator clanged on outside. Serge occasionally ran it for the time necessary to charge his flashlight and the old car battery wired to his radio. I crawled from beneath the mosquito net, shuffled down the hall with my laptop, and plugged it into the power strip.

Neither Serge nor his wife was in the front room, and

I sat, waiting deliriously. A bulky flying insect shot through the dark doorway—maybe a beetle of some sort—the buzz of its wings a low growl. Its carapace ricocheted off one wall and then another, before it streaked at the single hanging bulb and vanished past it, back outside, into a silence that left me blinking at the blue spots in my eyes.

I stood and walked into the twilight, feeling stronger in the cool air. I passed the pipe above the concrete basin and went to the trail. Far below, the river was visible, condensing the glow of the Milky Way into an astral path that meandered through the forest. Behind the trilling of insects, the water hissed faintly as it pulled against grass and reeds.

I hadn't been there long when the generator shut off. The immense, deep, and soothing darkness of the rainforest submerged me. It seemed louder now—a pulsing continuum that, as I turned to go back inside, became like silence.

"There's something I didn't tell you," Jasmine said as we lay on the floor. We'd had sex twice, the first time quick and the second, fifteen minutes later, long enough for me to feel some pride. Now she stared at the ceiling, her fingers knit below her breasts. I was content to lie there, looking at her.

"What?" I asked softly.

"My stepfather," she said, "when he came into my room that night, he put his hand in my underwear. He put his finger inside of me."

The sound of her breathing paused as she swallowed. I didn't say anything. I was afraid she wouldn't finish the story, though I didn't know if I wanted to hear it.

"He told my mom he was checking if I was a virgin. He thought I might be having sex with André, so

he wanted to check. I mean, it's bullshit. That's not why. He was always looking at me. Every time I came in the room. Anything I did. He was always there. It's so stupid, but that's what he said, and my mom believed him.

"André was the only friend I had. We could talk for hours. He told me how much he'd struggled and how hard things had been, how he'd considered killing himself when your mother left him. I told him that I wanted to move out and get away from my stepfather. I was unhappy, and so was he, and we'd sit in his room and just talk, and then, when I heard my parents come home, I'd run to my room."

"But you were eighteen," I said. "Why didn't you move out?"

She lay perfectly still, not glancing at me.

"I was fourteen," she said. "I'm eighteen now."

"And your parents let you move out with my father?"

"Yeah. He said he'd send me to school and take care of me. My mom didn't want me around. She said it was stressful with my stepfather, and I was happy with André."

"Did you go to school?"

"No. I didn't want to, and he didn't think it was important."

From across the river, the small ferry had drawn close, its engine humming. It docked with a clatter of metal and chains, and we lay as if listening for them, for some detail in the ruckus of waiting cars starting up their engines.

"I was sleeping with André," she said, after such a long pause that she seemed to be alone, speaking into the silence. "I was his girlfriend for four years."

I was trying to breathe—to decide if he'd put me

here to test one or both of us, or because he didn't care, or just to make me a man.

"What happened?" I asked. "Why are you here?"

"When you came back, he made me live here."

I cleared my throat to speak, as if that would give me words.

"Promise me," she said. "Promise me you'll never tell him what we've done."

"We can run away," I told her. "We can take the money from the till and go."

"No. We can't." Her words were soft, without authority, and yet final.

"Why? Why do you stay here?"

"Because I love him."

Each time the fever released me, I wrote until I had to stretch out again.

As a child, when I read, I was alone with each word vibrating with lifetimes of accrued meaning, with centuries of knowledge. The entirety of inaccessible adult civilization resonated in the ritual and incantatory construction of sentences, in what was said and what wasn't, in the way the characters were not so much expressions of themselves but of forces that had long existed among humans. They coalesced in words to take faces I too could wear as I became both particular and immeasurable, witness to a distinct life and imbued with a greater energy.

My father would come into the doorway and stare with restrained rage. My hands were latched onto a book, my eyes with an unconscious dilation that is the forgetting of limits, and my body flopped on the sofa, forgotten, in suspended animation, paused as my brain downloaded. My somatic neurons had connected to an imagined body, one that could encounter distant landscapes, that could escape.

Two days later, the phone rang.

"How are things there?" he asked.

"Fine," I said, and he was silent a long time.

"Are you and Jasmine getting along?"

"Yeah. We're fine."

To my own ears, my voice sounded shrill, distinctly adolescent. He was briefly silent, as if this were a test and I should know what to say next, or he was simply measuring the panic in my breathing.

"Anyway, I've planned a fishing trip for us in Squamish, where we used to go. I've been busy with the market, but I want us to do something together."

Squamish was a town on the river by that same name, an hour north of Vancouver. When I was little, before my mother and I had left him, it had been his favorite place to fish.

The next morning, he picked me up in the dark. We drove until a single lit fissure appeared high in the clouds above the mountains. Dawn saturated the mist as we followed an unpaved road. Trees and crags filled into their outlines. The radio was off. Beneath the wheels, wet gravel compressed with a sound like static.

A high embankment of earth and stones appeared, and he parked.

We prepared the fishing rods. I had the one he'd used when I was a kid, with a few missing eyelets. I tied on a spinning lure.

From behind the seat, he pulled a sweater and raincoat. He took off his leather jacket and button-down.

His biceps stretched the sleeves of his white undershirt, and the veins on his forearms and inside his elbows were swollen. He looked down, turning up his palm. Scars crossed it. A few were thick and pale over the web of finer ones.

"I always worked," he said, studying the bulging veins. "That must be what made them like this. In the pen, the junkies said I had good veins. They were jealous. They'd dig needles in their arms, but I stayed in shape. Nobody there wanted to fuck with me."

I was sure this was a threat.

We walked along the dirt road toward the embankment. In places, I could see where a bulldozer had pushed the rocky earth up the incline, leaving the deep striations of its blade and the faint imprints of treads. The road climbed to where a cable was locked to two posts, and we stepped over it and crested the ridge.

The river spread out, wide and shallow and fast. Hundreds of boulders broke its current, each one crowned with ice.

20

WHITE

The fever came and went with a rhythm I couldn't predict, except for dawn and dusk, when it burned most fiercely. Each time it surged through me, I felt my hatred of weakness—not only of sickness but of my constant, churning mental anguish—and with that hate came a memory of my father who couldn't speak the word "sick" in reference to himself, who would sit alone, staring at the wall in fury, waiting it out, trapped.

Even healthy, he'd never seemed comfortable at home, prowling from the bed to his chair in the living room, scowling at the news on TV, and then leaving to manage the businesses he'd started—a seafood store and a Christmas tree lot. His jeans, when I hugged him goodbye, smelled of pinesap and fish, of gasoline and sweat.

The only time we spent together was for work or occasionally fishing for leisure. Working with fish was respectable, he often told me, adding that our family had been fishermen for generations, though he hadn't spoken to them since before my birth. He took me fishing for trout and salmon, and we crouched on sunlit boulders as the silhouettes of steelheads, some longer than my body, passed through pools.

The only time I'd seen him gentle was with his dogs and cats, and that was once they'd been trained. He'd told me that only animals would never betray you.

As I rested, waiting on the strength to write, the bright spaces of the old mansion were the luminous backdrop for my memories.

The current was wide and shallow and fast. We made our way to the shore over icy river stones, carefully placing our feet. I stumbled, the lure jangling as the rod struck the ground behind me. My father glanced back, narrowing his eyes.

We each found a place and began casting.

Staring at the rushing water made me dizzy, giving me the impression that it was motionless and the boulders were perpetually floating past.

Every now and then, for a minute or two, the sun lit up fractures in the overcast sky, revealing strata of fog and cloud. Mist broke from the forest across from me and slowly glided along the river like large, pale birds.

We'd been there two hours. Thirty yards down the shore, he took in his line and looked at me. I couldn't make out his eyes. He stared and then returned his attention to the river.

I cast and reeled in, not caring about catching salmon, simply hoping that Jasmine hadn't said anything.

Sleet began to fall. He fished as if he didn't notice. The numbness in my hands made me a boy again, wanting his strength, his resilience to the elements.

Eventually, he turned and walked back toward the truck, and I followed. We hadn't been at the river for more than three hours and neither of us had caught a fish.

On the drive, we stopped at Kentucky Fried Chicken. He sat, tearing the meat off chicken wings and throwing the small bones on the white tabletop.

"Do you miss being a criminal?" I asked, my face feverish in the warm air.

"Sometimes. I made a lot of money and did whatever I wanted. But it couldn't last." He picked a drumstick out of the box. "I always thought I'd do one big job and then be free."

He'd told me this before—how, as a young man in Montreal, he'd learned safecracking and was arrested while jacking a sporting-goods store. In prison, he'd realized that serious criminals dreamed of the big job, the crime that would make them rich forever.

As he bit the meat off the drumstick, he stared me down. He swallowed and flicked the bone on the tabletop.

"Has anything happened between you and Jasmine?"

"No. Will you stop asking?" I said, scrunching up my face. I didn't know if he'd be angry, if he was trying to trap me, or if he saw her as some sort of bonding, and I was betraying him by lying—pushing him away.

He dug for another piece, a chicken wing that he snapped in his teeth. He spat a sliver down before us and glared at me as if I might disapprove.

Strewn with small broken bones, the table looked like the floor of a cave.

He wiped his fingers on wadded napkins, tossed them down, and walked out.

"Shouldn't we clean up?" I called after him.

"Fuck 'em," he said. "That's what they're paid for."

I went out and washed my face in the water from the pipe. I faced the sun, and my drying skin felt as if it was contracting against my bones. Briefly, I thought about how my life would appear, measured by the words I left, if I died here.

My strength having returned slightly, I walked alongside the narrow rill that ran from the pipe down the sweeping incline. The river resembled a dark shore before the pelagic expanse of the forest. The landscape and its watercourse seemed at a great remove, like something in a book.

The eastern horizon had begun to dim with the shadow of a storm.

Slowly, I made my way back to my room.

Days passed without a visit from my father. I told Jasmine how I hated him and his fish, how I would steal money from the snack bar and run away. I tried to convince her to go with me, but she didn't answer or even look at me.

Before her, I'd had sex once—quick and nearly pleasureless in the tall yellow grass behind my high school, near a chain-link fence. Now, each time she and I had sex, I sensed the promises of adulthood at last. But often I wasn't sure that she'd ever desired our intercourse. She could lie for hours with me on the couch, not kissing, just cuddled against me, as if for warmth. "Do you want to make love?" I'd ask, and she wouldn't even answer, so that after another ten or fifteen minutes, I would ask again, and she'd say, "Can't we just stay like this for now?"

Other evenings, she refused even to touch me. She would come downstairs and sit on her heels in front of the tree, just staring at it. As I lay on the couch with a book, I studied her shoulders beneath the thin lines of her nightgown's straps.

I paused between paragraphs to watch her, trying to make sense of what I felt for her—the intensity of my desire that I thought might be love—and I wished she'd stop feeling bad so we could have sex. That she'd been my father's girlfriend frightened me—she'd told me of the times he'd beaten her or thrown her out and made her spend the night in the street—but though these stories horrified me and I willed my lust to diminish, it didn't, and eventually, the next night, after cuddling for hours, she'd concede to my caresses.

As we undressed, the air around us felt electric. We were always listening, always apprehensive, and when cars neared the ferry, we paused, and I lifted my head, her hands slipping from my shoulders, lingering on my elbows. Sometimes, afterward, she would return to her contemplative position in front of the tree, and I would study her naked back: the fine shapes of its muscles just beneath her skin, the vulnerable curve of her spine, and the slow passage of her breath. Seeing her like that, without her observing me, seemed more intimate than anything else we'd done. On her knees, she faced the tree, silent, as if praying.

A week later, the gravel crunched outside. I knew it was my father from the speed at which he'd pulled into the driveway, the sudden braking. She raced up the narrow staircase to her room. Outside, the truck door slammed shut, and the sound of his feet came up the steps fast. Then he was standing in the doorway, looking at me where I lay on the couch with a book. She came down into the kitchen, having changed with impressive speed out of her nightgown into jeans and a T-shirt.

He looked from her face to mine and then back.

"Come outside," he told her. "I want to talk to you alone."

She put on her boots and jacket, and followed him out.

The door closed. I stood, crossed the room, and took the knob, but paused, frightened that I would turn it and then finding myself turning it. I stepped outside.

They were almost to the truck, their backs to me. He spun to face me.

"What are you doing? I didn't tell you to come out."

I just stood, opening and closing my hands as fog eddied beneath the streetlamp at the ferry docks.

He glanced at her and at me, and asked, "What's going on between you two?"

"Nothing," she said in a shrill voice.

"Get in the truck." He pointed behind him without looking at her. There was no expression on her face now as she obeyed him.

I came down the stairs and he stepped close. He raised his fist. His jaw clenched.

Without thinking, I began repeating, "I'm your son."

I didn't know where the words had come from—spoken between short, hurried breaths.

His eyes scoured my face.

"I'm your son," I said. "I'm your son . . ."

His expression calmed ever so slightly and he lowered his hand.

"Go inside," he told me, and I did.

I sat on the couch, my hands in my lap. An hour passed, maybe longer.

When she came back in, she held a box of black garbage bags. He was following her, and as he shut the door, she spun and shouted, "I don't have to listen to you."

Without hesitation—as if he'd expected this—he grabbed the front of her shirt. The garbage bags hit the floor, and the fabric at her collar tore as he swung her around and slammed her into the door. He punched the wood next to her head and then caught her by the throat, pinning her there.

"I'll get a gun," he told her, "and I'll come back in here and blow your fucking head off. So you do what I tell you."

He released her. She took a few steps and bent her knees, almost mechanically, to pick up the box of garbage bags. I was watching her face, but she didn't glance at me. She went upstairs. He stood, staring at me as I avoided his gaze. Bags of clothes began tumbling down the stairs.

When she came back, he said, "Everything. Put everything you own inside."

She was moving slowly now, as if exhausted, and he lunged, jerking the bag from her hands. He threw music cassettes inside and then cleared out the bathroom. I was pretty sure he'd thrown in my stuff as well, and I was thinking about my toothbrush and knew how stupid that was, but my head hurt.

He opened the front door. The night flooded the rooms with cold as, one by one, he swung the bags above the steps and onto the gravel.

He caught her arm and pulled her outside.

"Where are you going?" I asked, wanting to see her face, to know what she was feeling or thinking, but she was behind him, blocked from sight.

"It's none of your fucking business," he told me and slammed the door.

I'd been sitting on the couch the entire time. I stood and took a step, but stopped in the middle of the empty room. My bottom lip began to tremble and I closed my eyes, as if to hear the source of the motions in my body. I clenched the muscles of my arms and chest and jaw until I was still.

I went outside. The truck was gone. A hard, crystalline snow had begun to fall, sticking to the frozen ground, covering everything. No cars were waiting for the ferry, and I walked to the landing and stood beneath the single lamp. After a while, I lifted my gaze. The snowflakes fell past the shining glass, crowding my vision, burning against my skin.

A wind had blown up, carrying the fragrances of the forest, drifting them through the house: pollen, loam, mud, and decay, but also the musk of a living force I couldn't name. I breathed this new air, envisioning myself drawing power from it, healing.

But when I got up and went to the door, the wind slammed into trees, shook down dead branches, and whipped grit and pebbles into the air before breaking against the concrete walls. It shoved into my chest with corporal familiarity, as if inviting me to fight.

The sun was setting fast, and normally, just before dusk, my fever worsened. I was flushed and sweating now—a hot perspiration that felt like my body's triumph. I knew

I should rest and not exhaust myself, that I should change clothes to keep from getting a chill. But when I returned to my bed, I picked up my laptop.

After those weeks at the ferry crossing, I moved constantly, renting rooms or staying briefly with my mother before continuing on to the next place. I bought a car and slept in it on the nights that I couldn't find a couch. When I thought of Jasmine, I recalled the way we'd lain in the dark, just holding each other, the warmth and comfort of our bodies in that small house on the frozen edge of the river.

I kept my father at a distance. The last time I saw him, I was eighteen and had been accepted to a college in Vermont. Knowing it might be a while before I returned, he asked if we could go fishing. He'd aged suddenly in the previous months. He entered rooms tentatively, studying them before taking a step. He carried himself with tensed shoulders, as if protecting an injury.

It was a more clement December when we drove to Squamish. We followed the same gravel lane and parked. We attached our reels and then stood before the headlights to thread the rods.

As we climbed the embankment and descended to the shore, he took his time, finding his footing between rocks and driftwood. He stopped and looked around, at the wide, silver river, at the mountains whose stone faces burned in the slanting light.

"This is what we should've always done," he said. "It's all that mattered."

The sadness in his face was too clear, too uncomfortable for me, and I also looked off, at the landscape of stone and evergreens, as I breathed the cold air that moved over us, swept down from the mountains. I waited for him to keep walking.

At the end of that day, after our drive back to Vancouver, he parked next to my car, where I'd left it in a supermarket lot. He shut off the engine and lights. Rain had begun to fall, rattling faintly on the cab's metal roof.

"I know I did some things wrong," he said.

"What? What are you talking about?"

"With Jasmine."

I hadn't expected to speak of her again. Three years had passed since I'd left the ferry, since he'd loaded her belongings into black trash bags, put her in the truck, and driven off. He'd said only that he'd dropped her off somewhere in the interior, near where her family lived.

We sat in the truck, staring ahead.

"Why did you take her away?" I asked.

"What else was there to do? There was no future with her. We were never going to have anything. That's why I put her there with you. What happened didn't really matter. It shouldn't have mattered."

"I don't know what you mean."

"You saw her. I couldn't have started over with her. I couldn't have had a family with her. She wasn't . . ."

He fell silent, and I asked, "She wasn't what?"

"She wasn't white," he said.

Cars passed on the highway, the glow of their headlights moving over our windshield, illuminating the rain that flowed in rivulets before us and warped the light in the cab so that his face, when I glanced at it, looked as if underwater.

"Our children wouldn't have been white," he said. "They wouldn't have looked like you."

I tried to recall her. I saw her differently now. I didn't know why I hadn't seen her that way before. Having lived in Virginia, I'd come to think of race as a divide. She'd been white to my eyes, but there'd been something else in her, dark lineaments—different from me, maybe indigenous or Latin, and this seemed to explain why he'd been able to take her when she was fourteen, why no one had stopped him or asked.

I felt the full horror of what he'd done and of my part in it. But though I could almost make sense of what had happened, it remained incomplete. I was left with horror but no understanding, and I feared I would spend my life searching to explain it.

The fever knew that I was done. As soon as I lay down, it reclaimed whatever territory it had lost. The rest of the night felt interminable: blazing phosphenes, colors swirling beneath my eyelids.

The storm was just arriving. Tottering, I made my way to the window. The moon stared down between clouds that billowed, muscling upward like volcanic ash plumes. Trees swayed as the swollen wind fell against them, chipping away big leaves and hurling them down like scraps of metal from an atmospheric collision.

Then it was dark, the white, determining eye blotted out, and rain fell, pounding the walls. Water scraped at the exposed earth as if to hollow out the world and make it hospitable only for seas.

After flying back from Afghanistan the last time, I chose to live in New York City because I could stay in one place and still feel as if I was traveling. I could be among others while anonymous, interacting while alone. The largely manageable mania that had compelled me through years of projects overseas had given way to exhaustion. The dream of purpose dissolved. My story was a thread strung through emptiness.

Of course, somewhere within me, an instinctive will to live refused the absence of meaning, compelling me into motion. But each time I faltered, I found myself looking backward—revising decades in light of these vivid, brutal moments, these intersections with an earth unadorned by my delusions of the future self I was becoming—and then editing them together to understand the life I'd actually lived. I'd spent it chasing figments while the forces that drove me remained implacable, as insoluble as the universe itself.

My father had taken his own life two years after I'd moved away. He'd been dead twenty years, and I was still editing, still compelled.

21

RICHMOND HEW

After the absolute night of the storm—the density of the forest's darkness and of the unelectrified concrete around me—the clouds passed, revealing a halogenic moon. Its light bore down on the mist rising from the trees. Fever coursed beneath my skin. It seemed to me that the delirium had preceded the illness—that it might have preceded even the Pentus, though I couldn't recall. I found its packaging, holding it in the moonlight to reread the warnings. The letters danced in my head.

Pentus Pensut Petsun Neptus Netsup Pusnet Pestnu
Sentup Nestup Tensup Stepnu Sutnep Setpun Sutpen

I wanted to tell someone I was sick. Technology lived as a memory in my body, the ghost limb of an active smart phone, the feeling that my thoughts should be in constant conversation with those of others. My lost world was a dream of the future beneath an ancient moon.

I might have dozed. It was still night, and I wasn't

sure how the awareness came to me of the person in the room—a noise maybe, the sound of a door opening and closing, or just the air displaced by it—but at some point I sensed a presence.

I barely had the strength to prop my head up on my arm. A figure sat in the room's single wooden chair, facing me. He wore rain slickers, as my father often had, but he was bigger, paler. He didn't move, his head lowered in contemplation and his expression dark, unlit by the moon above the windows. He bent forward, dipping his face in shadow.

"You're awake," he said, or at least I think he did. "I know my time is up. Even if I keep delivering what the foreign donors want, I'm not sure how much longer I can survive out here. It's just a game now. But this is my life. It ends when I leave, so even a few days or weeks—they count for something. I will take action for them."

"Is that what happened to the others?" I asked, certain I was dreaming, inhabiting the malarial Hooke, sick and sweating in the same bed—now seeing through his eyes in his final hours.

"You mean, did I get rid of them so I could stay longer? There's no point in denying that, at least not to you. Terra learned about the diamonds. Keeping a secret here is hard. People will sell anything, and secrets are valuable only to the first buyer, so you must sell fast. That's how I've learned so much about you. Many little birds have come to me, asking for shiny things. But Terra, unlike you and the others, she was truly great at what she did. And yet her system couldn't last. She was a hero for being white in Africa. For not being so afraid that she stayed home. The rest is icing, since being white here is far safer than being black. The

Congolese know the impenetrability of our skin and the vulnerability of their own. But as I said, I admired her. She understood that power isn't a zero-sum game, unlike many white women, who compare every oppression others suffer to those they've faced, and who believe that doing so is a form of solidarity. All this is to say that I respected her. She was fully aware of her power, so who am I to blame her for using her pallor or sex as armor, or as a weapon, or even as a reward? She did what she had to do to achieve her goals. How many people can say that? I just would have preferred that she left my secrets alone."

Hew lifted his face out of the shadow, its large, blunt features the ones I'd imagined while reading Hooke's description of the Keeper. The refracted moonlight in his blue-white irises gave the impression that an incandescent process had ignited in his brain.

"And what will you do now?" I asked.

"As usual, I will do what must be done."

The way he said this didn't frighten me. Maybe I was too feverish, or his presence was simply familiar—similar to one I'd survived in the past.

"What happened to Hooke?"

Hew said nothing, just stared with those bleached irises, before lowering his face back into the shadow and speaking on in his lumbering yet decisive voice.

"Alton. He was a functionary. A bureaucrat. In his heart at least. Suffering through the guilt of those who've been protected. Dreaming he was a conqueror. Reading Cormac McCarthy in the Congo."

"That should be the title of a book," I said, suddenly no longer so certain that I was awake, my brain in a delusional swoon.

"You think?"

"Yes. A self-help book for men."

"Maybe," he said. "I found him odd, to come to a place with so much quiet suffering and read a novel in which death is strung out luxuriously over hundreds of purple pages. I read it after him. It's not bad, but it says so much about America and why I can't go back."

I could imagine Hooke's justification, that real literature was about suffering and violence—raw and unapologetic.

"Why do you want to stay out here so badly?" I asked.

"We all want things badly. Think of America. All those years of killing and torture to build the biggest, whitest cotton cocoon into which white people can burrow deeper and deeper. They kill to stay inside that . . ." He hesitated and then half-cleared his throat, half-coughed, with a wet dragging sound. "I was recently reading a book by this fellow—Jonathan Franzen. Have you heard of him?"

"Of course."

"So he's well known?"

"Definitely."

"Ah. Okay. Anyway, it reminded me of Gabriel García Márquez, of magical realism."

"Are you serious?"

"Very. That doesn't make sense to you? The writing is quite magical. Unless America has changed. But I can't imagine a world like that, where all the pointless little aspects of people's days have so much meaning. Where everyone's dirty little private lives glow as if they are radiating the light of God, and a marital spat or a family dinner is charged with the expectation of divine redemption. Franzen is writing fables of the white suburbs, perhaps even gospels . . ."

"I never imagined you as a reader."

"It's how I've survived so long out here. I'm not a hermit, though I imagine many hermits bear the contradiction of reading the words of the societies they reject. But often, those whom we read are those whom society rejected. The best books prevent us from feeling alone on the fringes. But, yes, I do read, and often. I actually got my hands on an e-reader loaded with books recently. Someone who came into the forest . . . Well, I guess we could say it got left behind."

"When did you last go back?" I asked, again starting to believe this conversation was real, that I couldn't be inventing it.

"Almost ten years ago, for a week," he said, "when I renewed my passport, before I realized that I didn't need to believe in passports out here, or visas, or anything like that. Money could solve it all. I do have connections with people, with organizations, of course, and I do occasionally get online. I'm not a Luddite. I just like it out here. Besides, if I were to go back, I'd have to learn how to use Facebook and Instagram and Twitter. And I've heard that Snapchat is a brain fuck."

"Don't bother with Snapchat. We're both too old."

"Really? What's it like?"

"It's hard to say. I've tried to use it, but my brain just locks up."

"Interesting. You've confirmed my suspicions."

"But who knows? I believe that the messages vanish pretty quickly. In theory, there's more privacy, so maybe you'd like it. But the other social media apps are intuitive. If you've managed to survive out here for so long, you'll have no problem."

"It's kind of you to say that, despite our conflicting interests."

"And what are our conflicting interests?"

"You want to leave here with a story about me that would destroy not only my way of life but my legacy. I want to be the one who controls my legacy."

"Then you should definitely get on Facebook."

He was silent, maybe deciding if my response was a joke. I wasn't sure myself, so feverous that I was trying to keep from blinking, afraid this conversation would end, that I'd fall asleep or wake up. My eyeballs felt dry and itchy and were beginning to burn. Maybe I was already dead, staring endlessly at nothing, and this idiotic conversation was my last delusion, the final string of misfiring neurons.

"I do what I do," Hew finally said, "because in the Congo, I get to be a white man in heyday America."

"That's it," I said. "The girls."

He shrugged. "You may as well take what you want. All these trends of sensitivity will pass. The human race changes enough that there will be future eras in which we will all be remembered kindly. But appetites are powerful. No matter how we repress them, they will triumph. Each group's liberation comes, driven by its desires. Someday we will liberate even the people we now consider monsters. It will be their turn to be humanized, and we will celebrate them by finding their horrors within ourselves. All of our parts will reside together. I understood this when I arrived, when I tasted what people here mean when they say power is eaten whole. Have you asked yourself why you keep coming back, why you must travel to places like this for your investigations? You are a lord the second you step off the plane."

There was a long silence in which I drifted in the fever's current. And yet I was asking myself who he was when he arrived thirty years ago, and how he'd changed—if his misuses of power had begun little by little, permitted by his scant pigmentation, learned one at a time until he unlocked his deepest fantasies of power. His documents—if I could find them in his jungle lair, the final circle of my descent—might show his own descent not so much into madness but into the freedom he'd granted himself to do anything.

"I read Jack Kerouac when I was kid," he said. "After that, each time I struggled to give myself permission to act on my desires, I picked up *On the Road*. Here was a guy who'd beat up gay people for sport with his friends. Sure, he felt bad about it later. And he did plenty of gay things himself. But he had sex with black prostitutes or Mexican prostitutes, and he and his friends even had sex with underage prostitutes and he wrote about it in the legendary brothel scene in *On the Road*. Tens of thousands of teenage boys have drooled over that long, drug-fueled car ride into Mexico, where Kerouac and his friends stopped at a brothel and took turns fucking teenaged Mexican girls. Maybe that's precisely what it takes for the institution to make you into a legend. So why am I not also a hero? The double-standard is absurd. If Kerouac had included a photo of that brothel scene in the book, then every hipster in America who buys *On the Road* could be put on the sex offender list, wearing ankle bracelets with GPS chips."

He let out a deep, lethargic laugh and shifted closer in his chair, its legs scraping the floor.

"But Kerouac was the freest white man in the world, wrapping up a book that is a celebration of freedom by envying black people. Do you know the scene? He's bone tired as he walks through Denver's colored neighborhood, and he feels regret at being a disillusioned white man. He says that he wishes he were a Negro—that the white world couldn't offer enough ecstasy. I read this page over and over. It's the whitest thing. To want it all. You take everything but the scraps of life and then romanticize even the scraps, imagine the pleasures of hardship, want the creative outpouring of the oppressed, their songs of grief, of urgent joy. We lay claim to their victimhood and their heroism. We—the good white people—want to be the saviors, since we have always been saviors of something, without quite knowing what we were saving. Even when we were killing them off in great numbers, we did it to save something. And now, after all that, our road is bigger and whiter than even that of Kerouac, the great jazz lover who surely believed he was one of the few white men to have understood black people. So it makes sense that his road has brought us here."

I felt overcome by my hatred of Hew right then, and though I wanted to speak—to indict him with questions—I was suddenly afraid, and in that pause, he continued.

"None of us are above each other—not you, me, Terra, or the Africans. We will all write the final version of ourselves as if we have achieved goodness. You see, I've thought about this a great deal—all the usual questions about mortality and what we leave behind. I've come to where I am now through a long process of questioning in which I have preferred brutal authenticity to the playact of enlightenment. Consider this. If, from some remote but glorious future, you were to write the present, how would you describe yourself? Hardly as the enlightened being you might consider yourself to be in that yet unimagined future. You would create a story of discovery, disillusionment, and self-betterment, and to do that, you would need a past self to sacrifice on the altar of error and ignorance so that you can be redeemed. The journey to our present righteousness, I realized, is always a lie that enables us to remain what we are—to exist with the illusion of ascendancy but without actually transforming. We read endless screeds on self-improvement not to change but to feel and tell others that we have changed. Goodness is a trick of perspective, a glimmer of virtue measured out against the infinitely more immense and more honest human darkness that we label animal or evil as quickly as we can, for fear that we might recognize ourselves in it, before we blank it out. You can spend your life dreaming innocence, or you can accept what you are and live."

He lowered his large head. Against the moon's pale light, his face sank back into shadow, but there was something confounded about his posture, the way he put his hand on his skull, his fingers dawdling along his scalp, as if he were trying to remember or to connect with himself in the recognition of a purported truth.

"You're a psychopath," I told him, my anger muted by the fear that he was right, that I was no better, that we displaced our casual racism onto the invented characters of our past selves, brought down punishments, delivered epiphanies, while, largely unchanged, we, the authors, go free.

He hadn't moved since I'd spoken, and from the shadow came a sudden, disjointed laughter, the likes of which I might expect from a cartoon ghost.

"Even being a psychopath," he said, "is a privilege that we have reserved for white people. Witness our favorite movies of the evil white masterminds, the cannibal geniuses and the like. Witness the great hunts for the white man who has gone over to the other side, whose very existence threatens our faith in civilization. Our characters chase across the earth for these fallen angels, but, like one of those awful Paulo Coehlo novels—in which the clichés have been even further blunted—you return home to what you've been seeking, having traveled only to find yourself. Rarely do we give the mythological power of true evil to black folks, because the white psychopath is our . . . I won't say it. Tell me. What is he? We all know."

There was a noise. He stood, lifting his face out of the shadow. Even in the dark, his eyes were crystalline. His gaze moved from me to the window with a slicing motion.

There was the sound of a truck engine on the road.

Headlights flashed across the dust-coated windowpanes, illuminating the empty room and the dark rectangle of the open doorway.

22

BACK IN ROOM 22(2)

"I am sorry, my friend."

The voice was Oméga's. Men were lifting me out of the bed, carrying me through the warm, blustery dark, to the back of a white Land Cruiser.

"What about the trees blocking the road?" I said, my voice dry and brittle.

"That was a hoax. The hotel owner deceived you so that you would stay and pay for more nights and more food."

I now lay on the floor of the Land Cruiser, Oméga watching me from outside. I was vaguely conscious of the hands of the men with him—moving confidently, positioning my body, covering me with blankets before lowering the hatch.

As the truck jolted over the uneven road, the silence of the cab recalled the safety I'd sensed as a child, on nights when my father drove us home from somewhere, or, later, when I slept in my mother's van on the long journey away from him, to Virginia, where we would start a new life.

I stared up through the truck's back window as the moon broke from the clouds. The trees on either side of our path seemed to rear back, exposing the long, wan paling of their trunks. I'd generated so much emotion over Serge's ruse—an innovation in tourism, the height of the tourist trap. But maybe Hew had paid Serge to lie to me, so he could observe me, or wait until I was sufficiently weakened from my illness. The fever had started after the first meal. I might have been poisoned.

I didn't know which of my mind's contents I could trust, or whether Hew had been but a manifestation of my fever.

When I woke, a transparent plastic tube ran into a sunken vein, blue and bruised in my arm. Dingy curtains hung around me. I lapsed again, blinking, and the metal bars on the sides of the bed vanished. An avocado lay on the windowsill. The sun flipped past the glass, faster and faster, catching up to the years between the war and now. Sola was washing my face with a cloth, her lips moving. A buzzing seemed to emanate from the narrowing canals of my ears.

When I opened my eyes again, the room was silent. Oméga, in a dark suit, was sitting in a chair, in the familiar configuration of a bedside visitor.

"When I was a young man, we all aspired to be white," he said, smiling and already well into the story, so that I wondered if I'd been awake but without consciousness. "Maybe for you, for whom whiteness is a very pure thing, you cannot see my Belgian blood. But understanding my small inheritance of whiteness was a struggle of my youth, before I renounced it. Still, it is sad not to be seen for what is part of you.

"Before the war, when I was in university, I had a chance to work briefly in the Virunga National Park, during the vacation. Only the best students were chosen for an internship, during which future conservationists might be selected to be trained. There were some young white men, students from abroad, and I recall one night, after we'd all been doing a study in the forest, the whites arranged some chairs in a half circle and began drinking as they watched the sunset. If they had been village elders or Congolese, it would have been normal for young people to gather around and observe—even if at a respectable distance, in the event they were discussing something important. But most of them were my age, so I went over and pulled up a chair. There was a bottle of gin, and I reached for it. I'll never forget the sound one of the men made. 'Ahem,' he said. 'Ahem. Please don't.'

"'But why?' I asked, and he said, 'It's for us. It's not easy to find here.' As I studied the bottle, another of the men said, 'We're just sharing a moment among ourselves, mind you.' I replied, 'Yes,' but without understanding what they were saying, and he added, 'I mean, would you mind letting us share this moment among ourselves? Sometimes it's nice for us to have some quiet time alone.' And then the other said, in a voice that sounded very false and defensive, 'Well, it's about having more training. It's a career issue. We're further along.' I said, 'Oh. I see,' like that, so that it sounded as if I understood. The fellow said, 'You do? Good. Well, I'm sorry, but we need our moment. You know, this isn't our country. It's not easy. We come here, and we need a moment that feels like home. It doesn't feel like home if everyone's here with us.'

"I was confused, since I'd received the same internship as several of them, but I left. I never forgot that—how they turned me away. I had to sit and think about it. Those weeks, no matter how I tried, I wasn't able to engage one of them in conversation. It's such a simple human thing to converse, to exchange stories and see who is before you, and yet, with them, that was nearly impossible.

"It took me years to place that experience in history. My father had talked about how his own father was an *évolué*—a member of a special class invented by the Belgians and comprising the most successfully colonized blacks. It could be joined only after the whites had evaluated the African as sufficiently evolved in his ways—that's to say, sufficiently white. But his own father was the son of a young woman who was a maid in a Belgian house and who—mysteriously in the eyes of the white woman she worked for—became pregnant even though she rarely went out. It was only natural that the Belgians opened such a privileged door to one who carried so much of their blood. But with independence, when the Simbas—the Maoist Tigers—rose up, they began slaughtering the *évolués*. The Belgians fled or were saved by foreign soldiers, while my grandfather moved his family from town to town, making them bake in the sun for hours every day so that no one would see their whiteness, though of course these things are very hard to hide. Hearing these stories, I came to understand that the rewards for trying to be white were small compared to the punishments.

"Maybe that is how I have come to this point, still at war—in a matter of speaking—with whiteness. I am faithful to God, and my spiritual calling comes first, but since I've been asked to serve my country, that too must be His will. I have listened, and the divine has told me to drive out the men who won't."

He tilted his head, evaluating me.

"I need you to get better and write the story about Hew

and Terra—all of their madness. No whites will believe it if I tell it. That is still the state of the world, no matter how much I resist it. When I take over Hew's projects, the big organizations will complain. Many of his admirers will accuse me of being a corrupt and inept African. It is infuriating. For generations, whites have told us that we must do things their way, while accusing us of doing things our way—or at least what they imagine to be our way—while they secretly do things in the way that they denounce as our way. And yet they always benefit. Now I will do things my way. All you need to do is tell this story so that white people understand the truth the only way they can."

I tried to say more but my throat was too dry. I closed my eyes and when I opened them, he was gone. On the chair was a stack of documents.

One morning, the lightshows, echoes, and burbles in my head ceased. I propped myself up and slid my legs over the edge of the bed. My knees looked bulbous, swollen, but when I felt them, they fit into my palms the same as before. The rest of me had simply been greatly reduced. The power was out, and I stood and made my way to the bathroom, and peered in the mirror. The face that hung deep in the glass looked stripped of all authority, estranged—thin and creased and shadowed.

An image of Hew returned to me then, the moon's luster at his back and the way he'd lowered his face into his shadow, as if drinking from it. Even as my white eyes had glowed with these details, they'd struggled not to read centuries of delusion into a simple moment, not to infect the elementary gradations in luminance with symbols, with histories of ascendancy and primordial pasts—myths of the animal being anywhere but here. The shadows have always been our own: a mere conveyance of the most basic laws of physics, of bodies blotting a neutral light.

When I returned to the bed, I began to skim the pages which, by then, Sola had shifted to the nightstand. They included allegations against Hew for smuggling, statutory rape, giving and receiving bribes, as well as testimonies from village chiefs about his behavior with specific adolescent girls and numbers I could call in Kinshasa to speak to people who would verify the charges. There were photocopies of slips of paper registering sizeable, inexplicable payments to ministers, police chiefs, and members of the military. There were legal testimonies accusing Hew of involvement in the murder of Terra and her driver, as well as a number of Congolese names I didn't recognize. There was a sheaf of poems—Baraka's, I realized—many of the pages maculated with the pale pink remnants of blood, and a note from Oméga asking that all of Hew's casualties be included.

I closed my eyes and when I opened them again, it seemed to me that the room might not be the same one I'd been in before leaving for the east—that my perspective on the parking lot had shifted slightly.

I began compiling my notes from this trip—all that I'd heard and read over the past weeks, in language that verged on clarity but never quite arrived, as if I stared through fog, expecting it to lift, though instead it fell like a shutter, more blinding than the night.

Sola dropped by each evening, warning me to go slowly, making sure I'd eaten, that I hadn't forgotten to take a variety of pills. She told me that the doctors had cast a wide net, unsure of why I hadn't been responding to the medication. She still hadn't found the girl and talked a little about work, but I was in a manic concentration. She spoke as I struggled to be present, and eventually she fell silent. "Working like this isn't going to help you recover," she told me as she was leaving, and then added, "I didn't come here to be your caretaker."

During the day, I paused from writing to call Oméga and ask questions. He was often too busy to answer and no longer visited, but he had his secretary send me names and numbers as well as documents. I recalled his story about being an intern in Virunga and realized that his position as minister of the environment wasn't a sinecure, that he must have a past that intersected with Sébastien and likely even Hew—that he might be making himself scarce now so the investigation wouldn't lead back to him.

But even as I gathered my notes for the exposé, it was the writing of these pages that gripped me. I composed them inexhaustibly, it seemed, inspired by a frenetic energy, only to collapse suddenly into sleep lit with vivid fever dreams. I had a sense of being lost, searching for something, turning and turning with the certainty that I would soon know. I woke from one dream, recalling the impression I'd had reading the girl's testimony of the white demon—that Hew had somehow intersected with her. Though I tried to dispel the notion of an emergent whole, the idea grew. I quelled the thought only by telling myself that I would need to speak with her regardless, for the article about her. I called the pimps more regularly, offering more money.

As I worked, the power went out often—the result of repairs to the electrical system, the clerk told me when I called reception, and then, the next time, of problems with the hydroelectric dam. So I paid him to print these pages: my writing, these notes, the found documents, the transcripts of interviews. I fit them together like clippings into a collage. I spread the pages across the floor of the hotel room, many torn at points of insertion. Seeing the snippets of paper and text, I had the impression that I was in a plane again, looking down upon the map of my life.

Exhausted, I dropped onto the bed and slept, before waking suddenly in a cold sweat and returning to work—making these annotations or handwriting links, often while lying on the floor, as I had when I was a child. In my struggle to recompose the various voices that had led me to this moment, I returned often to the pages in which I'd tried to reconstruct my conversation with Hew. His arrogant, sordid jabber still resonated in the depths of my skull, a lingering vibration as I labored to recall his precise words, to separate them from my own and give them sense. I deleted and rewrote, increasingly certain of his presence in the room with me but not of the exact shape of his savage and absurd formulations.

The pages I most lingered over were those about my father. When I was a teenager, the few times he'd asked me if I was dating anyone at school, he said, "If you bring a girl home, make sure she's blond. You don't want to risk having babies that don't have blond hair and blue eyes." I didn't understand his obsession and thought briefly of the flaxen-haired princesses in the stories I'd read as a child, or the golden locks of pop culture sex icons. He was dark—nearly as dark as Jasmine—and years later, while reading Henry James, I ran across lines referring to the impoverished and uneducated mass of French Canadians as brown people. I'd lingered over this—explored it, researched it, and learned how much indigenous blood the French Canadians had, and how ashamed of it many had been. Their English conquerors saw them as an inferior race, as mutts without a real language, and, fearing they would ruin the country, pressured them to assimilate. All the while, the Catholic Church rallied them toward a different European culture, with the goal of preserving their language and faith. More and more francophone Canadians defined themselves as *hommes blancs* in opposition to the indigenous peoples they resembled in many ways. Eventually, nearly half the province's population of impoverished French speakers immigrated to the US, where they were told to "speak white" and had to further assimilate, often changing their names or becoming Protestant. Among those who stayed behind, the majority were the manual labor—the impoverished farmers and factory hands—for the Anglophone ruling class, *les nègres blancs*, as some called them.

With the urgency of self-hatred, my father had broken with his family. A man with dark hair, dark eyes, and olive skin, he'd rushed out of a culture that was colonial in its attitudes toward the indigenous people while itself enduring the oppression of British colonial rule. He'd experienced the racism of North America and the racial divisions and hierarchies in American prisons, and he'd understood the power and the promise of whiteness. In the way he'd looked at me and in the times he'd said he wished he could be me, or look like me, I knew I was the fruit of his success.

When we'd spoken of Jasmine and he'd said, "She wasn't white," the very idea of whiteness had shifted in my mind, and I realized that he—perhaps without realizing it—had been struggling to attain it his entire life, and, having been accepted as a white man, had seen the prize of his whiteness return in the form of me, not only estranged but also disparaging his life. Jasmine had been his lesson in power, his way of showing me what we were and what held us together.

My life before that experience seemed a tabula rasa, the blank slate of childhood, a time when my forays and reinventions embodied hope and possibility. I had been certain that when I got myself right, the world would affirm me.

One afternoon, the telephone woke me. It was Oméga, explaining that his ministerial appointment was keeping him busy.

"When I have a calm moment," he said, "we will meet for dinner."

"That sounds good," I told him, not certain whether his offer was sincere and there had truly been some friendship between us.

"I just want thank you for everything," I said.

He was silent longer than was normal for a phone conversation, so that I instantly found myself trying to determine if I'd made yet another misstep.

"There is no need to thank me," he replied, speaking softly now. "I know this may seem strange to you, but I do not exist to provide lessons to foreigners. I chose to facilitate your work for a reason. We are both doing our jobs and we both have had our objectives all along. This is the nature of human interaction and does not preclude goodwill, though you whites always assume that we blacks will serve you from the goodness of our simple hearts and, when we don't, you see it as a grand conspiracy. I cannot imagine the pain of losing the justifications for outrage and righteousness. Of course, I am not blind to the irony that even in telling you that I am not here to provide lessons to *mundele*, I am providing one. Such is the lot of the earth's black people, to go from building the edifices of whites with the wealth of our labor, to being responsible for their moral edification."

Later, I woke lethargically from a deeper, more exhausted sleep than in the previous days, to the ringing of my cell.

"I have the girl," a gravelly voice said in French. "When do you want her?"

"Now," I told him. I gave him the name of the hotel and said he should call again when he was outside. I rang Sola and told her to hurry back.

And now I wait, staring at these nearly finished notes, jotting these words on them, uncertain of what to add, how to complete this story that isn't what Oméga hoped for. Soon, I will have to strip these scenes to their pith and start over—be a journalist and reduce all of these pieces to a single story whose narrative is unified and concise, told within a single voice.

But for now, the feeling I have is one I sometimes experience in moments of completion, when what I've been holding or searching for is about to be released. As I let go, exhaustion comes over me, similar to the feeling of expenditure after being with a lover—an emptying out, a brief, effortless existing, without purpose or direction—and then, within that hollowness, a seed of new awareness. What I thought would satisfy or complete me wasn't as monumental as I'd dreamed. No horrors have been diminished or destroyed. I am once again adrift.

AFTERWORD

BY SIMISOLA BATTA

In the preparation of these posthumous pages, I have tried to remain faithful to Béchard's translations of the people he met—not just of their words but of their bodies, their ways of moving through the world, since all of the above are, in his depictions, foreign to me: not ill intentioned but simply of another worldview, informed by a highly structured and teleological sense of existence I do not share.

Since people cannot record the moment of their deaths, I will attempt to describe Béchard's. There is little to narrate, since he recounted his life in writing as close to his own end as one can hope: a writerly finish by all standards.

I had just pulled up in a taxi. The pimp, a burly man wearing wraparound shades, held the girl by her arm. She was struggling to get away, and I heard her say something about *le démon*. Then her head snapped up and she focused on a hotel window. Béchard was standing close to the glass, only two floors up but high enough for his presence to seem dominant and menacing. Briefly, I felt as if I were seeing through her eyes: the ghostly figure hovering above us, imbued with all the power of one who looks down on another from a height. Even the way that Béchard vanished from the window was ominous. A figure that stares down at you without fear, before quickly disappearing, is one who is coming to get you.

The girl began kicking and screaming, and when the pimp picked her up in a bear hug, trying to immobilize her, she bit his wrist and he dropped her. She ran, but he caught her tangled hair, jerking her back.

I was shouting for them to calm down. I can't say why I chose to crouch or show her my palms. This seemed a primordial way of proving I had no intention of harming her. The big man had her in his clutch again. Her neck twisted as she looked at me. Her eyes were very blue, their whites visible all around.

At my request, he put her down but kept a firm grip on her forearm.

Then she turned from me, as if, without looking, she knew Béchard would be close. He was. He'd come out of the hotel lobby and was making his way toward us. She lifted her free arm, pointed at him and, with her index finger extended, raised her thumb. Closing one eye, she squinted the other, carefully taking aim.

Though the gesture was that of a child's game, its intensity and determination were not. She'd gone tense all over. She was thin, her skin cleaving to the bone, and in that moment, with her every muscle taut and lifted, she appeared like a tiny athlete, her body mercenary to her will.

I looked from her to Béchard as he walked closer. There was something unusual in how he moved. One of his feet dragged a little, and his hands were behaving oddly, no longer swinging in motion with his step but trembling, fluttering in brief intervals. Suddenly, they went rigid. He stopped, staring transfixed at the girl, and shook as if with fear, as if playing along with her game.

I knelt next to her and spoke soothingly, but she didn't look at me, didn't for a second take her attention from him. I'd never seen such single-mindedness in a child, and I began to feel afraid. Her right eye narrowed to a slit, sighting past her finger, and then she brought her thumb down. Béchard dropped to his knees. I heard his bones hit the concrete. He fell onto his face.

I will pause here to say that all my life I have not known what to believe. Those who have strong faith in their mystical maneuvers repeat them again and again until finally an event confirms their power—and that is enough. Béchard did fall, and later, in the hospital, after the autopsy, the doctors said that a particularly aggressive and drug-resistant strain of falciparum malaria had gone meningitic, attacking his brain. Though he had been recovering from a more standard malarial infection, the parasite had somehow crossed the blood–brain barrier. As in many cases, once the attack begins, death follows quickly. And yet it's strange that he had the strength to walk out of the hotel. Though I know it to be a coincidence, I am haunted by the simultaneity of his final moment and the girl's thumb coming down.

After Béchard's death, the Dutch anthropologist Bram Rees published his now rather famous paper, "The White Witch and the Demon of Whiteness," in which he argues that Béchard had internalized a worldview similar to the girl's—had somehow, over years of travel, become sensitive to other cultural perceptions and visions of power. Rees describes his encounters with Béchard and how, when he told stories of Luna the White Witch, Béchard's eyes grew moist and he rubbed away goose bumps on his arms.

Rees, in a rather strategic narrative twist, asserts that he himself is in part responsible for Béchard's death, allowing as he did for Béchard to take home and reread Luna's testimonies. In this way, Béchard fully internalized them, especially during a period of exhaustion, loneliness, and worsening illness—"when," in the words of Rees, "the fragile psyche could no longer protect its cultural worldview." Rees goes on to make the following argument:

> *Béchard's belief in the White Witch's power (and perhaps even a certain identification with the demon she was destined to destroy) infiltrated, took root, and grew quickly during his periods of dementia. Just as the tribal citizen who reveres the powers of sorcerers may become ill upon learning that a curse has been cast upon him—dying simply because he believes in its power—Béchard so utterly gave himself over to his cultural appropriation that his biology obeyed his beliefs, and he fell before his terror of the White Witch.*‡

---

‡ Rees, "The White Witch and the Demon of Whiteness," published in the *New York Times Magazine* (November 12, 2017), excerpted from *The Demon of Whiteness* (forthcoming from Simon & Schuster, with material original published in and adapted from *The Journal of Experimental Anthropology* (Cambridge, 2017), 22–23. Rees also heavily references "voodoo death," the term coined in 1942 by the American physiologist Walter Cannon, though Rees speaks of the term as psychosomatic death—the death of the body as the result of an emotional response heavily rooted in a traditional belief system.

To say that I disagree with Rees would be an understatement. In the preceding pages, I have seen no evidence for his theory, and I hope that the publication of these notes will clear up such misconceptions or any harm that Rees's mythologizing and self-promoting may have done to Béchard's legacy. However, I should note that Rees was not incorrect in presuming that the girl had Western films in her heritage. After Béchard fell, she lifted the tip of her index finger to her lips, so that it was pointing at the sky, and blew on it.

At the hospital, when I met Pastor Thomas Oméga, he expressed his bereavement and asked if I would be willing to help compile Béchard's documents or find a journalist who would do so. I agreed and also reached out to Daniel Slager, the editor of his books. We ultimately worked together to present this text in its current form. Material from it and from the copious other notes that Béchard accumulated were used in support of the exposé published in *Mother Jones*, "Big Conservation's Scramble for Africa," written by Ellen Hernandez, though Béchard was included as a coauthor in the byline.

I don't know whether Hew left the Congo or stayed, or even whether the news of his fall reached the remote area where he dwelled. I spoke with Oméga, who believed that Hew had retreated into the deep forests with his reserves of cash, to live out his days as a *Mokonzi* in a secluded village. I learned that Oméga had taken over the management of the country's parks and conservation projects, making TV appearances in the role of pastor—preaching about Eden, the creation of the earth, and man's responsibility to manage and protect God's gifts in the natural world.

My final weeks in the Congo were largely spent trying

to find the girl again. In the confusion after Béchard's collapse, she escaped. I had my driver call the pimps and passed my days on the roads of Kinshasa, looking out the window and paying street children for any tips they could offer.

On the afternoon that I found her, a powerful rainstorm had just blown through. She was with another girl, the two of them huddled like sparrows in winter sunlight, on the edge of a cemetery.

Though it took some time, I befriended them with food. The white girl's name was Delia, a far cry from the mythic appellation Rees gives her in his stories. The black girl was Marvine—tall for her age, thin, with wiry, twitchy muscles and a curiosity about everything. While Delia kept quiet, Marvine pointed to my necklace, my ring, my shoes, my hair, asking questions.

Eventually, they came with me to the hotel. I bought them new clothes and fed them continuously to remove any desire they might have to rush into the street, and I was surprised to see them curl up in the bed and sleep for nearly a day.

When they woke, I cuddled with them. I was careful not to lose their attention for a second. I scratched their backs and styled their hair, and we spent hours in the bathrooms, scouring each dirty toe that I then painted whichever color they chose. Having read Rees's notes and the story of how the demon washed Delia's color off in a bath, I was afraid she would resist bathing, but she didn't.

They spoke to me in Lingala and bits of French, but it was clear that Delia understood English. She was shy about speaking it, and though I knew that with patience I would unravel her story, it wasn't my priority. I simply hoped to forge a bond and win their trust.

While they slept, I called people at the embassy and hired Congolese acquaintances in the government here and friends in the US to help expedite the process of adoption, even as the embassies did their best to turn up information on a missing white girl, though with no luck.

A week of nuisances did follow, with a Congolese police officer dropping by and telling me the girl should be charged with murder and imprisoned, or at the very least burned in the street to prevent her demon from infecting others. I resorted to calling Oméga, who put an end to the problems with the police while expediting the adoption papers. He offered to have Delia exorcised in his church before my departure, but I declined, and then, before saying goodbye, he warned me to be careful with her. After that, he no longer called or visited.

Those nights, as the girls slept, I reread Béchard's notes. His quest is hard for me to define—the way he ceaselessly measured his life in abstract terms rather than set concrete goals. He appears to view the latter as futile but, oddly enough, not the former. The artistic act is his yardstick, the apogee of individuality, even though it leads him into a current of whiteness in which he is less character than scene. As a white man trying to step outside of whiteness while on the whitest of quests, he evokes an avatar denying divinity while proclaiming his own coming.

There is also—it would be unprofessional not to disclose this—an emotional component to working on these pages. I have done so finding myself wishing that Béchard had been able to reveal more about himself not only in them but also to me. And yet I relate to his deep sense of dislocation, the failed bond to kin that leads to an urgent need for a larger connection—to fix what was broken in the family, but to do so in society. This impulse, while gravitating toward a sense of universal kinship, contains the risk of delusion, of seeing oneself as a savior.

Even as Béchard agonized over his place within the conflicts of colonialism and class—and recognized the ways in which they are inflicted on women's bodies—his concerns around identity and the obscurations of whiteness consumed him to the point of blindness, to the degree that he spent more time contemplating his place in the universe than he did the systematic rape of black girls by a white man.

Even in an encounter like the one I had with him, he struggled to see me. He couldn't ask about my identity, nor could he unburden himself of needing to know. The result was that even this small unknown took on a glimmer of fantasy—once again the eroticism of discovery, despite his intentions. He kept trying to strip back his preconceptions and projections, until the very idea that he had to do so with me became, in itself, a palimpsest of sorts. In this way, it seems appropriate that he first saw me partially masked and tried to read knowledge on my body before I even woke, noticed him, or spoke to him. And yet, perhaps his failure as a boy to discern Jasmine's racial traits and understand their significance had scarred him, and his mission in life, whether conscious or not, had become to unsee what he couldn't help but notice everywhere. As a result, my character often appears less a complete person than an allusion to his past—the foreshadowing of a resurgent memory.

Ultimately, I can't find myself or Oméga, or any of the others with whom Béchard spoke, in his words. He appears to have had so much to say that he had to enlist every person he met to say it, even as he integrates the white narratives he encounters—those artifacts of genre and professional methodologies for which his own becomes a sort of integument.

Despite what he reveals, Béchard remains a white man on his journey of self-discovery into the other, with the clichéd trappings of colonial encounter: exotic lessons from magical men (at the cost of one of them dying), sexual adventure with an unreadable woman (yes, me), and a rite of passage in which love and rape are inextricable. There is no forgiveness at the end of his story, simply more appropriation. Like Rees, he sees himself mirrored in the people before him and is quick to express all that he has learned from them, before he reaches for the next character that he will make his own.

As for Hew, who embodies not wisdom but the cold knowledge of how the world works, he appears less a monster than a source of fascination, a key to Béchard's inner struggles that he never fully reveals. The victims fade from sight, and the eye turns with eagerness—if not cloaked admiration—to study the face of the perpetrator.

As for Delia and Marvine, their adoption papers came through, and I bought tickets to Boston, where my mother now lives and had scheduled a battery of medical exams for both girls. Delia and Marvine seemed content with me. We watched movies, and they ate so ferociously and constantly that they appeared to grow visibly.

The harmonious stillness stayed with us through the ride to the airport. They were awed by the clean insides of hotels and new cars, and touched everything, whispering to each other. They didn't even glance out the windows at the lives they were leaving behind.

On the plane, after takeoff, the girls settled down. I

was drowsy, with Delia cuddled against me on one side and Marvine on the other, and we all fell asleep.

When I woke, the sun was rising, and Delia faced the window, staring out at the plane's wing. Tears streamed down her face.

"What's wrong?" I asked.

"The knife," she said in English.

I looked out at the wing that, drenched in morning light, gleamed like a blade.

Maybe, I thought, it is better to remember the life you have imagined, to retain some of that magic and hold its creative power for the future.

But then she whispered, "Demons . . ."

And I realized where I was taking her.

ACKNOWLEDGMENTS

Thank you to the following for encouragement and support during the writing of this book: Austin Lin, Bonnie Huang, Mark Preston, Emily Goldman, Heather Slomski, Frani O'Toole, Sarah Dougherty, Ashley Mitchell, Nancy Romer, Lew Friedman, Dominique Fortier, Antoine Tanguay, Erica Mason, Kevin Lin, Graham Moore, Arthur Moore, Kevin Williams, and my mother, Bonnie Ellis. I am grateful for the support of Canada Council for the Arts, the MacDowell Colony, and the Writers Room in Manhattan. This book was informed by the research and writing of many scholars and journalists, among them Filip De Boeck and Michela Wrong. Special thanks to everyone at Milkweed Editions—in particular, Mary Austin Speaker for the cover design, Joey McGarvey for her work preparing the book for publication, and Daniel Slager for his support and editorial advice.

DENI ELLIS BÉCHARD is the author of five other books: *Vandal Love*, winner of the 2007 Commonwealth Writers Prize; *Cures for Hunger*, a memoir about his father who robbed banks; *Of Bonobos and Men*, winner of the 2015 Nautilus Book Award for investigative journalism; *Into the Sun*, winner of the 2017 Midwest Book Award for literary fiction; and *Kuei, My Friend: A Conversation on Race and Reconciliation*, an epistolary book coauthored with First Nations poet Natasha Kanapé-Fontaine. His work has been featured in *Best Canadian Essays*, and his photojournalism has been exhibited in the Canadian Museum of Human Rights. His articles, fiction, and photos have been published in dozens of newspapers and magazines, including the *LA Times*, *Salon*, *Reuters*, the *Paris Review*, the *Guardian*, *Patagonia*, *La Repubblica*, the *Walrus*, *Pacific Standard*, *Le Devoir*, *Vanity Fair Italia*, the *Herald Scotland*, the *Huffington Post*, the *Harvard Review*, the *National Post*, and *Foreign Policy*. He has reported from India, Cuba, Rwanda, Colombia, Iraq, the Congo, and Afghanistan.

milkweed
editions

Founded as a nonprofit organization in 1980, Milkweed Editions is an independent publisher. Our mission is to identify, nurture and publish transformative literature, and build an engaged community around it.

We are aided in this mission by generous individuals who make a gift to underwrite books on our list. Special underwriting for *White* was provided by Barry Berg and Walter Tambor.

milkweed.org

Interior design by Mary Austin Speaker
Typeset in Caslon

Adobe Caslon Pro was created by Carol Twombly for Adobe Systems in 1990. Her design was inspired by the family of typefaces cut by the celebrated engraver William Caslon I, whose family foundry served England with clean, elegant type from the early Enlightenment through the turn of the twentieth century.